They had broken through and flooded into the castle just as she had sat down for a rest.

She had not had the time to gather her gloves or headgear, but had been caught in the flight downstairs where she now fought back against as many of the enemy as she could.

"Nooo."

A keening cry of fury rent the air around her, turning the hairs on her arms up into panic as her eyes caught sight of the one she had thought never to see again.

Marc!

Here.

In the mail of King David, sword tipped red.

A traitor and a betrayer; a man who would leave the keep of Ceann Gronna with secrets in his head to return a brace of months later and use them against those who had only been kind.

A payment of death for the gift of life. She could smell the sea spray on him as he jostled closer, his eyes cold with the knowledge of retribution and deceit.

* * *

Lady with the Devil's Scar
Harlequin® Historical #1102—August 2012

Lady with the Devil's Scar

SOPHIA JAMES

HARLEQUIN®

entertain, enrich, inspire™

Recycling programs
for this product may
not exist in your area.

ISBN-13: 978-0-373-29702-3

LADY WITH THE DEVIL'S SCAR

Copyright © 2012 by Sophia James

www.Harlequin.com

Printed in U.S.A.

For the Chelsea Bay Book Club...
my group of warrior women.

Chapter One

1346—Fife Ness, Scotland

Isobel Dalceann saw the shapes from the beach, beyond the waves, turning in the current, dark against silver. Eight or more of them, lost in the grey swell of stormtide as mist swallowed outline.

'There,' she shouted to the two men beside her. 'Two hundred yards out.'

The Heads yielded an odd wreck of a boat sometimes or the carcase of a sea creature long since dead...but this? Dusk spread from the west, burnishing lead with a blushed quiet pink and changing something that was not known into something that was.

'People!' Ian voiced the knowledge first. Not wood or fish or the trunk of a tree that had slipped into the brine somewhere near Dundee before travelling south in the cold currents, but people. People who would drown unless she helped them; she had always been a strong swimmer.

Stripping off brogans and tunic, she removed the dirk held by straps against her ankle and ran.

The water took her breath before she had crossed the first waves, long beaching swells with the chill of the northern climes on their edge; when her hair knotted around her arms, forcing her to tread water, she rebound it tight.

Ten yards away Ian shouted and Angus responded, the next breaker lifting them all and aiding direction. She could hear the beat of blood in her ears as the wash took her under. Counting the seconds to surface, she kicked her feet hard and broke through just short of one of the survivors.

An open cut from elbow to shoulder bone wept red into the sea, swirling in the foam before being lost to the great vastness of the German Ocean. He barely registered her presence as she paddled across, noticing for the first time that another lay beside him.

'I will take him while you swim in,' she shouted above the wind as rain started, each drop forming bowls on the surface, tiny pits in a boiling sea.

'No.' He held on with the tenacity of one who would not let go, green eyes steeled into resolve; as Isobel looked closer, she saw the man between them was long dead.

'He's gone. The sea has taken him.'

Shaking his head, he turned from her, shoulders

hunching into grief. The curl of his fingers tightened even as she watched, dimpled white and marred with bruises as he breathed in once and then twice, garnering strength and regrouping will. How often had she done the same herself, the loneliness of everything unbearable?

'Let me help,' she called, 'for the shore is far away.' Her touch against his shoulder roused him from his own private hell as he gazed at her with all the arrogance of one unused to direction.

Isobel pushed down a stir of unease. Even the few paltry moments that she had been in the ocean had chilled her and she wondered how these people could have survived for so long.

'H-help the others behind me f-first.' When he shifted his hand to cradle the head of the man he supported, a thick band of wrought-plaited gold lay at his wrist.

No simple sailor, then, plying the straits between England and Scotland to gain a living. His accent held the softer beat of another more foreign land.

A shout behind made her turn. Isobel saw that Angus panted with cold, his legs treading water with exaggerated hurry as he tried to keep warm. Fear struck deep. Two hundred yards from safety, with the rolling edge of a sea storm coming in from the east. Behind him two men were trying to rise on his bulk in their fight to gain breath.

Lord. The sea claimed its victims without recourse

to any fair play or just reserve. Swimming over, she clouted the oldest man hard across the head, breaking his grip and pressing against his throat, pleased as his eyes rolled into white. Then she did the same to the youngest.

'Que Dieu nous en garde!' Marc muttered. The woman with the scar from one side of her face to the other was killing those with him one by one and the chill that held him stiff with cold meant he could do nothing about it.

Guy was dead. He had known it all of an hour ago and still his fingers could not open to simply let go.

The water beneath him called, an easy rest and an ending, and the strength that had held him to the task of rescue was suddenly gone. He could not care. It was finished. As his fingers opened and his eyelids rested he felt the warmth that had long since been leached from his body return in a quick and bright light.

Scotland. His father's land. He had not quite made it.

'Hold him from behind,' Isobel instructed Angus. 'Do not let him turn for he will pull you down in his panic.'

'I cannae handle the both of them, mind.' Angus's words were thrown through the gathering wind.

'Then choose the youngest.' Such a choice out here

in a sea that was rising held no guilt for Isobel. The fittest would survive and be done with it.

But the green-eyed stranger was gone, too, pulled beneath the sea by lethargy, his red sleeveless surcoat with the bright gold braiding disappeared. She should leave him, of course, should take the advice she had just offered Angus, but a stronger force willed her to action. Diving down through the murky water, she saw him turn towards her, as if he had known she might be there, glances catching through the brine, the white of his skin the colour of death.

One last kick and she reached out to snag cloth before hauling him up into the dusk and air. They surfaced like a log might in a swollen mountain stream, a curtain of foam and salt lashed around them, rain stinging skin.

Thumping his back hard with the heel of her hand, she felt him take a breath, the rise and fall of his chest strong as he coughed, a hacking endless bark that dislodged the water he had swallowed. His hair lay around his face in tousled dark-blond tails, wiped back as he found breath in a hard movement, his lips blue.

Around her the cries of the survivors told another story. One stranger perished here and another there. They floated away with their faces down in the water, swirling as leaves in the current.

She could not save everyone with a changing stormtide on the turn for out. All the will in the world could not alter what happened to those too long in the hands of the sea as the heat of skin cooled and relaxed into death.

But the green-eyed stranger hung on through the breakers, his mouth tilted towards the air, the cold chattering of his teeth like a drum beat as they came closer to landfall. He was using his strength to help her, too; she could feel his legs move against her own until his feet found purchase on the ocean floor.

He was tall, then. Much taller than her husband had been before…

But she did not think of that as she brushed away anger and watched him stand, the sea to his waist now, every second showing more of a man who looked nothing like anyone from around Fife. Menace and danger lingered in the long bones of his body, the fancy surcoat with its plaited braiding belying the man beneath.

'I can m-manage,' he said abruptly and turned to watch her two men find the shore, each bringing with them a survivor from the stricken boat.

Three people out of eight, was her anguished thought. Lord God, that it could have been more.

The fierce desolation in his eyes told her that he also counted, though he was swaying with cold, tiredness and injury, the open gash on his arm pulled apart by the sea into a lengthy, grim, dark line on his upper arm. It no longer bled. Isobel wondered whether that was a good sign or a bad one.

'We are camped in the trees and there is warmth there.' She did not like the anxiety she could hear in her words, as though it might be important to her that he did live, but he was barely listening as he walked across to his friend and spoke softly in a language she recognised as French. Both turned to the line of bush behind them as if weighing their chances of safety.

'How is it you are called?' His voice was stronger now as he switched back to English.

'Isobel Dalceann. My home lies two days' walk west along the coast from here.'

She saw how his glance took in her sodden hose, tight about her legs, her ankles full on show. It had been so long since she had worn the garb of a woman that she'd forgotten that those who did not know her might find it odd. Without meaning to she smiled and saw the sting of it in his eyes. Her scar, probably. It always puckered badly over one cheek when she showed emotion.

With the night coming on, however, she had had enough. She had risked her own life and any criticism of what she looked like or dressed like would have to wait till later. There were rabbits skinned and trussed near the fire and a half-a-dozen fish wrapped in leaves beside them. Once they had eaten their fill and found blankets to shelter beneath she could determine just what it was these newcomers sought and how quickly she could be rid of them.

* * *

'Sacrée Vierge.' Marc could hardly place one foot in front of the other one as he came into the camp under the trees, his head spinning in a way that made balance difficult. Perhaps it was the blood loss or the cold or simply the near-transportation of his soul from this life to the next one, leaving flesh behind. He had seen it before on the battlefields in France, the astonishment of death greater even than the fear of it. The anger in him rose as he refocused on that about him.

It was dark beneath the cover of the canopy of trees and afternoon rain had left a dampness that was all-encompassing.

Simon looked as exhausted as he did. The other survivor's name he had no notion of, but fancied him to be one of the deckhands on the boat into Edinburgh. The young man shook so much that he needed to be carried between the arms of the two men who had swum out. Marc knew that he would not last long. The woman was ordering everyone around and the knives strapped to her ankle and belt were sharp.

'Where exactly are we?' he purposefully asked in French. The blank response confirmed what he had suspected. None spoke the language. He was glad, for it allowed Simon and him privacy to decide what to do.

'They are all well armed and we are both injured. We will need to wait for our moment.'

Simon nodded. 'At a guess I would place us some-where on the Nose of Fife just north from where the Firth enters the coast down into Edinburgh.' His hand ran across his upper thigh, a bruise seen through the tear in his clothing. His voice sounded rough. 'What do you imagine they mean to do with—?'

The question was cut off by the sudden intrusion of one of their saviours looming close as the cross at Simon's neck was ripped away. The ring on his fin-ger was gestured to next.

When he went to protest Marc stopped him. 'Wait. It is only the trinkets they need, after all; as payment for our lives, I'd deem it fair.'

Stripping his bracelet from his wrist, Marc placed it on the ground. As he did so he looked up and saw the woman watching him, a scowl on her face and anger in her brown eyes. She glanced away as soon as she perceived his notice and continued to tend to the fire and food.

Her hair had escaped its binding and fell in a sheer dark curtain to her waist. In the building flame there were lights of shot red amongst wet ebony and he was surprised by the want that surged inside him as he thought of what it might feel like to touch.

Shaking away such nonsense, he sat on the ground and leaned back against a tree, feeling better with the strong solidness of wood behind him.

'Where are you from?'

Her voice was hard, the frustration in it unhidden. He noticed she did not ask for names.

'France.' He had decided that there were only certain pieces that needed telling. 'The boat we were on was blown off course and overturned in the storm.'

Her attention was drawn to the other men beside her, their words rising in anger as they squabbled over the jewels. She stopped them with a short command, though the oldest of the pair drew his hands into fists and punched the air, twice.

Intentions!

Staying expressionless, Marc looked back at the woman. Her fingers had crept to the knife at her belt, relaxing as she saw one of her men move off into the forest, though when she gestured to the other to tie them up Marc swore beneath his breath.

He could fight, he supposed, and win, but with an arm that needed some attention and Simon with a leg that was taking him nowhere he thought it better to wait.

The rope was thick and well secured, putting them a good length away from each other. When the man was finished Isobel Dalceann checked the ropes herself. Her flesh was freezing as her arm brushed against her prisoner's and he thought for the first time that she was good at hiding her feelings.

'We'll unfasten you when the food is ready, but at every other time you will be tethered until we decide what to do with you. After dinner I will tend to your arm.'

Her last sentence heartened him. If she meant to kill them, surely she would not waste any time caring for them first? Then the import of what she said sunk in. The gash was deep and the light was bad and the few belongings seen in this provisional camp pointed to the fact that medical care would be at best basic.

'I can wait.'

His saviour began to laugh and there were deep dimples in both her cheeks. He heard Simon next to him draw in breath and knew that his thoughts were exactly the same as his own.

This warrior queen was the most beautiful woman he had ever seen, despite the scar and her garb and the grimace that was her more normal expression. Looking away, he tried to take stock of such thoughts and failed. Beneath his tight hose lust grew. God… the world was falling topsy-turvy and he could stop none of it. Shifting his stance, he bent his knees.

'Wait for what? Edinburgh is almost a week's worth of walking from here and by that time your arm…' She stopped, her teeth worrying her bottom lip. 'The sea may have cleaned it, of course, but the bindings holding you are well used.'

He frowned, not understanding her reasoning.

'It is my experience that filth often finishes what a blade begins.'

Riddles. Another thought wormed into his head.

Was she one of the silkies that the legends from these parts were full of? He had never seen a woman so easily able to manage the sea before and the colour of her hair was that of the sleek black coats of fur seals often sighted off the coastline.

Lord. The blood loss was making him unhinged and those knowing eyes so full of secrets were directing him to imagine things that would never come to pass.

He looked away and did not speak again.

The stranger would be screaming before the night was out despite the careful diction in his sentences. Isobel was glad for it, glad to imagine the weakness in him as he submitted to a mending that would not be easy.

He unsettled her with his verdant, vivid eyes, his high-priced golden bracelet and his French accent. Ian had wanted to kill him, finish him off and be done with any nuisance or trouble, but the thought of his blood running on the ground as his soul left for the places above or below filled her with a dread she had not felt before. They were probably David's men, newly returned from France with the fire of the power of the monarch in their bellies, and no mind for the ancient laws.

What would they know of her and of Ceann Gronna?

'Unmarriageable Isobel' she was called now; she

had heard it from a bard who had come to the keep with a song of the same name.

Swearing soundly, she returned to the food, panic subsiding as the everyday task took her attention; two days' walk to the keep and another two to Dunfermline where the strangers could be sent by ferry across the Firth towards Edinburgh.

She wished Ian and Angus had not been with her, for she would have to watch them and the foreigners at the same time. Anything of worth had been taken, after all, and now their presence could only be a bother. Isobel doubted the third man would last the night, given his colour, but there was little in truth she could do about any of it.

She hoped that the green-eyed man would speak the French again so she might over-listen and at least know just what his intentions were.

The jewellery might tell her something of them, of course, but she did not wish to ask Angus for a look at the haul just to probe into the mystery of who he was. Nae. Better she never knew and sent him on, out of her life and out of her notice.

The simple silver ring on her own finger tightened as she turned it, a lifetime pledge reduced to just two years, and then a yoke of guilt. Sometimes, like now, she hated who she had become, a scavenger outside the new system of government imposed on the old virtue of possession, leaving no true home in any of it. Even the ground did not speak to her as it used to, whispering promises of the for ever. Once the system of lairdship had ruled this place, the great estates handed down through the generations, like treasured possessions and always nurtured. Until King David had come with his fealty and his barons, taking the land by force and granting it to his own vassals for their allegiance and loyalty.

Now possession was tempered by blood and war and betrayal. Sweat beaded beneath the hair at her nape and if she had been alone she might have lifted the heavy mass away from her skin and simply stood there.

But she was not alone.

She could feel his eyes on her back like a hawk might watch a mouse crossing a field. Waiting.

Had he not said exactly that to his friend as he sat there against the tree, his hose tight in places that made the blood in her face roar.

'Alisdair.'

The name came beneath breath like a prayer or a plea, invoking what was lost and would never be again. She was glad when Angus reappeared from the forest with a bundle of dry tinder and a good handful of blaeberries.

Chapter Two

The fish and rabbit were tenderly cooked and when the one she called Ian might have given them only a very small portion she had gestured him to ladle out a full plate, with a crust of hard black bread in the juice.

The boatman had eaten nothing, his head lolling on to his chest in a way that was worrying. Marc saw the woman bring an extra blanket and lay him down on it with care. He also saw that she did not bind him again, but left him free. To die in the night without fetters, he supposed. Perhaps there was some folklore from this part of the world that a man should meet his maker unconstrained.

After she had finished with his comfort she came to him, loosening the ties at his wrists and directing him to come to the fire.

There was a flask of whisky waiting and she motioned him to drink. The brooding in her eyes lent him the thought that she had not meant to do this at all and he swallowed as much as he could before she took it back. He was pleased to feel the burn of it down his throat as an edge of calm settled.

He would need it. Already she had lifted her knife.

'I have to remove the bad skin.'

He had not even answered before she poured whisky across his gash, fire against the hurt and his heart beating as fast as he had ever heard it.

Flames lightened her eyes into living gold and her fingers on the blade were dextrous. He saw she had another scar running from the base of her smallest finger right across the foot of her knuckles to the thumb. He wondered if she had got that at the same time as she had received the one on her face.

'If you stay still, it will help.'

The message in her words was plain. Move and the agony will be greater. Like a challenge thrown down into the heart of mercy.

He wished he had a piece of leather to bite upon, but she did not offer it and he would not ask.

'You are experienced in the art of healing?'

At this question both the men behind her began to laugh.

'The art of killing more like,' one of them muttered.

He saw her grasp tighten on the blade, an infinitely small movement that suggested wrath a hundred times its size. He trusted it also signalled care or humanity or just simple expertise. At the moment it was the best he could hope for. Marc was surprised when she spoke again and at length.

'From experience I find healers are women with little mind for the ordinary. My opinion of them is tempered by their need to eke out some existence in a world that might otherwise be lost to madness.'

This train of thought was to his liking. 'So you are not of that ilk?'

'Witches and fairy folk are born into the lines that whelp them.'

As Isobel raised her blade into the light the dancing flames were reflected in silver.

'But your line was different?' Suddenly he wanted to know something of her. With her mind distracted by his pain and hurt, she might be persuaded to answer him.

But she remained silent, her lips firm as she cut into his flesh, the roiling nausea that had been with him since the rescue at the beach rising up into his throat as bile.

'Lord Almighty.'

'You are a religious man, then?'

'If I said that I was would it help my cause?'

'With your God or with me?' she countered, turning the knife into live tissue and watching as blood filled the wound.

He swallowed.

'There is sand and grit in the furrow and it must be removed.'

'Grain by grain?' He visibly flinched and she stopped for a second to watch him, a measured challenge in the tilt of her head and so close he could feel the warmth of her breath.

He shook and hated himself for it, but even as he held his hand to anchor the elbow to his side he could not stop it.

Shock, he thought; a malady that men might perish of as easily as they did the cold. On an afterthought he glanced over to the boatman on the blanket and saw that he had stopped breathing.

'He left us as I poured the whisky across your arm.' Isobel Dalceann's words held no whisper of sorrow even though she had tended him. 'Tomorrow would have been too hard for him to manage, so our Lord in his wisdom has seen him walk along another path.'

Two things hit him simultaneously as she uttered this. She was a spiritual woman and she was also a practical one. For some obscure reason both were comforting.

The pain, however, was starting to war with the numbness of whisky and he stayed quiet. Counting.

By the time he had got to a hundred and she placed her knife back on the hook across the fire he knew he was going to be sick.

She turned away and did not watch him throw up even though she had promised herself that she would.

But this man with his bruised green eyes and gilded surcoat was...beguiling. No other damn word for it.

As long as he did not look as though he might fall over and mark the wound with the earth she would wait; patience had always been her one great virtue, after all.

'Are you finished?' She wished she might have inflected some empathy into the query, but the others were watching her and they would not expect it.

Nodding, he straightened. He still shook, though not with the fervour that he had done before.

'The poultice I have prepared will numb any pain you have.' God in Heaven, now why had she said that?

A slight smile lifted his lips. 'Do I dare hope that the Angel of Agony has a dint in her armour?'

'The needle that I will sew your hide up with is not my finest.'

'Where is your finest?'

'Lost in the skin of a patient who had no time to sit longer.'

'A pity, that. Not for him, but for me.'

Unexpectedly she laughed out loud, as though everything in her world was right.

Ian stood and sidled closer. 'Have ye drunk more of the whisky than ye used on him, Izzy?' he asked and picked up the cask. Snatching it from him, she placed it on the ground and plucked an earthenware container from her bag. Sticks of fragrant summer heal and dried valerian were caught in twists of paper, but it was the rolled and cleaned gut of a lamb that she sought.

Taking the long sinew between her fingers, she wished the stranger might simply faint away and leave her to the job of what had to happen next, for no amount of alcohol would dull this pain.

With the needle balanced across the flame, she dunked the gut in boiling garlic water before threading it, feeling the sting of heat on her skin. A gypsy she had met once from Dundee had shown her the finer points of medical management and she had never forgotten the rules. Heat everything until boiling point and touch as little as you needed to. Alisdair had bought her silver forceps from Edinburgh after they had been married, but they had been lost in the chaos of protecting Ceann Gronna. Just as he had been! She wished she might have had the small instrument now with its sharp clasp and easy handling.

Her patient's arm glistened in the firelight, the pure strength and hard muscle, defined by the flame, tensing as she came closer.

'If you stiffen, it will hurt more.'

He smiled and his teeth were white and even. Isobel wished he had been ugly or old.

'Hard to be relaxed when your needle looks as if it might better serve a shoemaker.'

'The skins of all animals have much the same properties.' Pulling the flap of skin forwards, she dug in deep. The first puncture made a definite pop in the silence, but he did not move. Not even an inch. She had never known a patient to sit so still before and she kent from experience just how much it must hurt.

She made a line of stitches along the wound. Blood welled against the intrusion and his other hand came forwards to wipe it away. She stopped him.

'It is better to let it weep until the poultice is applied.' She did not wish to tell him again of her need for cleanliness.

He nodded, his breath faster now. On his top lip sweat beaded, the growth of a one-day beard easily seen, though he turned from her when he perceived that she watched him.

'The woman has the way of a witch. I do not know if we should trust her.' His friend spoke in French, caution in his words, but the green-eyed one only laughed.

'Witch or not, Simon, I doubt that the physic at court could have made a better job.'

Court? Did he mean in Edinburgh or Paris?

Flexing his arm as she finished, he frowned when the stitches caught.

'It would be better to keep still.' She did not want her handiwork marred by use.

'For how long?'

Shrugging, she took the powders up from their twists of paper and mixed them on the palm of her hand with spit. A day or a week? She had seen some men lift a sword the next evening and others fail to be able to ever dress themselves properly again. Positioning his arm, she placed the brown paste over the wound and bound it with cloth, securing the ends with a knot after splitting the fabric.

'By tomorrow you will know if it festers.'

'And if it does?'

'Then my efforts will be all in vain and you will lose either your arm or your life.'

'The choice of Hades.'

'Well, the Sea Gods let you loose from the ocean so perhaps the Healing God will follow their lead.'

She was relieved as he moved a good distance away.

Everything ached: his arm, his head and his throat. The rain from above was heavy, wetting them with its constant drizzle.

He slept fitfully, curled into the blanket like a child, waking only as the moon waned against the coming dawn. Isobel Dalceann sat upright against the trunk of a tree. Her hair now was bunched under a hat so that the raindrops fell off the wide edge to dribble down the grey worsted wool of her overcoat. One hand played with the beads of an ebony rosary, glass sparking in the fire-flames and the way her lips moved soundlessly suggested an age-old chant. He could not take his eyes away from a woman whose knife lay across her knees, ready to take a life after spending the whole of an evening trying to save one.

'I know you are awake.'

He couldn't help but be amused. 'Hard to sleep with the possibility of losing my arm on the morrow.'

'How do you feel now?'

'Sore.'

'But not sick?'

He shook his head.

'Then I should imagine you will get to keep it, after all.'

'Your bedside manner lacks a certain tenderness.'

She smiled. 'Ian hoped you might be dead by now. We placed the other man back into the outgoing tide and he'd like to do the same with you.'

'Unshackle us and we will walk away in any direction you choose.'

'The problem with that is you have the way of our names and our faces, and there are many who would hurt us here in the ancient hunting grounds of the Dalceann clan.'

'If we gave our word of honour to maintain only silence…?'

'Words of honour have the unfortunate tendency to become surplus to survival once safety is reached.'

'Then why did you swim out to us in the first place?'

Her eyes flickered to the empty skin at his wrist.

'The gold?' He pushed himself up to a sitting position. Streaks of red-hot pain snaked into his shoulder. 'You could not have known that we were adorned with such before you reached us.'

He caught the white line of her teeth. 'But we could hope.'

'Only that?'

She remained a shadow amongst the trees, her legs against her chest with a blanket around her shoulders. 'A boat left the Ceann Gronna keep two weeks ago bound south with a dozen of our men aboard and Ian, Angus and I came from the keep to see if we could see any sign of its return. We thought it might be the vessel that had foundered.' Her hand stilled for a moment on the count of the beads and she switched languages with barely an inflection of change. 'You spoke with your friend today of a physic at court. Which one do you hail from?' He was astonished.

'You speak French?'

'Fluently. My mother was from Antwerp.'

'It might have been wiser to keep that to yourself.'

'As a weapon?' Deep dimples graced each cheek as she placed her fingers across her mouth. For the first time since he had been in her company he saw the coquette she might have played so very well in any other lifetime. 'Why would I have need of one? Your friend can hardly walk with his bruising and your arm is bound and useless. Are you right-handed?'

'Yes.'

'Then let us hope you have had practice with your other arm to fend off the enemy.'

'Why? Are they close?'

'You are looking straight at one, *monsieur*. As close as breath.' No humour at all lingered.

'A woman who has saved me twice can hardly be classed as an enemy.'

'The most cunning of foes are those you know and trust.'

He knew she spoke from her own experience but, with a little chink of goodwill settling between them, did not wish to mention it and ruin the discourse.

Besides, here in the night with the moon upon them and the quiet call of birds that did not sleep, either, there was a sense of camaraderie he had never felt before with any woman.

'What is your name?' Her question came after many moments of silence and he hesitated. How much should he tell her? He opted for caution.

'James.'

She turned it on her tongue twice. 'I had a brother of the same name.'

He noted the past tense.

'My mother took him with her when she left my father. I was six. He was three. The boat they used to escape foundered off Kincraig Point and they were both drowned.'

Her head tipped up and he saw her eyes watching him in the moonlight. Why had her mother not taken her? He did not like to ask the question, but she answered it for him anyway.

'Enemies can operate under the guise of love just as easily as they can do hate, and it is my experience that all parents have their favourites.'

'God.' His expletive was filled with all the anger she must have felt as a six-year-old.

'Were there other siblings?'

'You ask too many questions,' she said and stood, stretching. The outline of one breast was easily seen against her tunic where the material had slipped to allow the soft abundance an escape.

Mon Dieu, he was turning into a man he did not recognise.

Was it the light-headedness after the doctoring that had him ogling a woman who might still be tossing him back into an outgoing tide come the morrow?

But there was something about her, with her long dark hair and her prickliness, a female set apart from others and fierce. He could not think of even one man of his acquaintance who would have braved such a cold and angry sea.

He also wondered how long she had lived rough like this, lost from society and the discourse of other women.

Her travelling companions lay over the other side of the clearing, their snores mingling with Simon's, a whisky pouch beside them, and an array of knives and crossbows against a rock at the ready.

Enemies. Everywhere.

The day pressed upon him with all its unexpected turnings. Guy lost, Simon saved and his arm sewn up by a woman who looked like a battered angel. With a sigh he closed his eyes and drifted into sleep.

She could hear him breathing, evenly, slumber taking over from pain.

He lay with his good arm tucked under his head as a cushion against the hardness of the ground, the drizzle sitting on his hair like small jewels. He was a puzzle, this James, with his careful green eyes and his golden bracelet and his way of making certain that all those about him were safe. She had heard the boatman and the one called Simon talk of the way he had rescued them from the trappings of rope and sail as the boat had foundered, clawing his way back to find whoever was left. The marks of bruises all over him told her that the task had not been easy, either, and his vigilance and guardedness here even in the face of pain was unrelenting.

Swearing beneath her breath, she balled her fists and listened to him take breath, quiet in the night and comforting. It was this comfort that had led her to speak of her mother, a subject she had not shared with one other person in all of her life. All twenty-three years of it. Lord, it seemed like so much more.

James. He didn't suit the name, she thought. Too proper for a man who looked as he did. Too very orthodox and prim. She wished he might wake up so that they could talk again out here in the night alone with the rain to shelter their words from the others, but the day had exhausted him and she was glad that he lay in the arms of rest.

She couldn't sleep because there were too many thoughts in her head, too many memories dredged up: her mother's sadness and her father's fury when he realised that his wife had escaped through one of the sea caves under Ceann Gronna. He had ranted and raved on the high battlements for all of the hours of the storm and when Isobel had gone to him to try to help he had pushed her away, screaming his hatred. Such recollections made her melancholy, a small child blamed for all the self-absorption and egotism of her parents.

She needed some space away from this stranger with all his questions inciting unwanted confidences she had never told another soul. Ian would not hurt them unduly for she had made sure he had understood the consequences should he fail to protect them.

Careful not to wake anyone as she packed up her things, she lifted a branch and disappeared like a ghost into the thickness of the forest.

Chapter Three

Isobel Dalceann was gone when he awoke next, the headache he had felt coming in the night now a pounding curse.

Simon looked about as bad as he felt, the shaking the boatman from Le Havre had been consumed by touching him now, and the red in his eyes as bright as blood.

The two Scotsmen sat by the fire, warming their hands across flame.

'Is there water?' Marc's question was directed at the younger man.

'It depends who'd be a-wanting it,' the one called Ian answered, his arm coming up to hold the other back from the task of offering succour. Angus, he remembered Isobel Dalceann had called him. The lad looked remarkably like Ian. Perhaps they were kin?

'My friend is hot…'

'Then a swim in the cool of the ocean might do

him good.' He rose now and sauntered towards them, malice drawn into the long bones of his body.

'I noticed a stream on the way here yesterday. That might do even better.'

Scowling, Ian changed the subject altogether. 'The insignia on the bracelet we took from you—what does it mean?'

'I picked the piece up in a trading city in the north of France. Perhaps it denotes a family connection or the acknowledgement of some property.'

'Or perhaps ye are here to spy for the king?'

'Philip the Sixth of France is too busy with his own problems to be burdened with those of Scotland as well.'

'I was speaking of David of the Scots.'

'As a purveyor of fine cloth newly come in from Brittany, I leave politics to the domain of those who understand them.' Marc made his accent subtly stronger and shrugged his shoulders to underline the point. Indifference held its own defence. It was the intricate little gestures that made a person believe in a ruse rather than the large ones. How long had he known that? With difficulty he stood.

'Cloth like that of your surcoat?' Angus's question implied interest.

'Indeed.' The scarlet velvet was rich in the morning light as he looked around.

'Where is the woman?' Trying to take any interest from the query, Marc knew he had failed when the other struck him full in the face. Reeling, he regained his footing, a trail of blood dripping across his left eyebrow turning the world red as the soldier's instinct in him surfaced.

'Isobel Dalceann is nothing to you, understand, for I saw the way you looked at her with the firelight in your eyes and want in your belly.'

The Scotsman drew a knife as he spat out the words; kicking out, Marc upended him, using the moment's uncertainty to kick harder. Long years of practice made the task so easy he could have done it in his sleep. When the man lay still, he turned to find the younger one gone, the water pouch abandoned on the track. Laying his bound palms across the smooth earth of the pathway, Marc listened to movements fading into silence. He made for their keep probably. Isobel Dalceann had already told him it was within walking distance of less than two days west.

Edinburgh lay in the very same direction, on a fortified inner bay of the Forth, at least four days' hard walk and Simon in no fit state to do any of it.

Grabbing Ian's knife, he held the blade against the rope at his wrist, sliding back and forth in order to break the bonds. When he was free he cut the ropes binding Simon. His arm hurt like hell at the movement and bright red spread across the bandage, dripping off his fingers in a slimy viscosity. Wiping them against velvet, he looked around. A crossbow had been left and a blanket. Beckoning Simon to collect them while he knotted the discarded ropes into a longer length, he bound Ian to a hefty trunk of tree.

Not dead.

Part of him knew he should pull back his neck and slit his throat here in the quiet of the glade and out of the sight of others, but Isobel Dalceann had smiled at this Scotsman in the way of a friend and there was some hesitation in him that was disturbing, some unfamiliar notion to please.

Simon was coughing in an alarming manner, the breath he took shallow and fast.

'I a-am f-freezing.'

Marc knew the opposite was the truth for he had felt the hot flush of skin as he had untied him. He stripped his tunic and the blanket away, then they made for the stream crossed yesterday back at the headland off the beach. His friend's shaking had worsened, the slight tremors giving way to an uncontrolled jerkiness which lessened a bit as Marc dumped him into the water and held him there. Resistance faded as cold ran across heat.

'God,' he muttered as the red in his own arm spread into the stream and Simon began to cry.

Biting down on her bottom lip, Isobel thought of the moment her life had changed, from one thing to the other and no chance of turning it different. Her hand lifted to her face and traced the edge of scar into the hairline just below her left ear as consequences settled across her like a stone. If she could go back two years she would have and if she could have gone back another five then all the better again.

So many damn years of war! They were etched into her face as hard lines of age. Alisdair dying by her father's hands, yet even as he had left this world her husband had incited mercy and pardon until blood dribbled down the side of his mouth, taking away words. Her father had always been unstable and she had spent much of her youth avoiding his heavy right arm. He hated her because James had gone and she was left, a daughter who looked too much like his 'treacherous wife'.

The anger that congealed inside her sometimes stymied breath and, stopping beside a tree, she hung her head across her knees, fighting terror.

It always happened like this, unexpectedly vicious, the regrets of a lifetime channelled to that one horrific moment with never any solace.

Fingering the silver ring on her finger, she was glad for it. Inside the band Alisdair had engraved the word BELIEF. She had wondered if he meant belief in God or in him at the time he had given it to her. Now she used the word to mark her life. Belief in what she was doing was just. Belief in protecting those still left at Ceann Gronna. Belief in the old rights of land law and clan.

She looked to the west. Clouds darkened the horizon and the rain was falling harder than it had in the night. The pathways home would be muddy and difficult and the time it took to get back to the keep would double in such conditions.

She had been gone for four hours already and the sun was up. She needed to get back to make certain that the strangers were shepherded out of the Dalceann lands. With grim determination she turned to walk against the wind.

She saw the green-eyed one and his friend from a distance on the slopes a good two miles from where they had camped, but Angus and Ian were not with them. Her head tilted to one side, listening. Where the hell were her men? Why had they let these two make their way unaided towards Edinburgh?

James had removed the scarlet surcoat and wore it inside out now, the dark satin of the lining blending into the colour of the trees. The one named Simon hung on to his elbow, more in hindrance than anything else, his limp pronounced.

With care, Isobel skirted into the bush, watching as they came up towards her. James saw her first. Congealed blood lay on the white linen strips she had protected his wound with and he carried the arm high against his chest.

As he smiled she swallowed down a sudden and inexplicable need to touch him and her breathing tightened.

'Where are the others?'

'The taller man is tied up in the glade we slept in—'

She broke over his words. 'Alive?'

When he nodded she felt relief flare in her eyes. 'And Angus?'

'Run off...several hours ago.'

His face in the light was harder than she remembered it to be and she saw Ian's knife tucked beneath his belt.

His glance took in the brace of pigeons she had captured on the incline at the Alamere Creagh before coming back to her face. She saw him frown before he turned away.

Isobel Dalceann was like the space between lightning and thunder when all of the world holds its breath for what was to come. A woman apart from others, incomprehensible and unexpected.

He wished that just for a moment she might be gentle or kind or vulnerable, might smile or shake her head in the way of one who was uncertain, might come forwards and offer solace to Simon.

But she did none of these things as she gestured them to follow, only minions in her wake as the forest closed in about them, holding back the bands of rain. The dead birds hung at her side like an omen.

His arm ached hot and throbbing and the weight of Simon pulled him sidewards. Even a fool could see that if a village did not come soon he was done for and Isobel Dalceann was far from a fool. They came down tall dunes of sand into a sheltered bay, butterflies and flowers bordering a stream.

'Put him here,' she said finally as Simon gestured he could go no further. Laying down her own blanket, she knelt at his friend's side.

Her hand ran across the injured leg and she felt the bruise rise up against her palm, the heat of infection surprising her. Last night this man had shown no sign of any injury save that of the ocean-cold in his bones and she cursed beneath her breath as she recognised her oversight. She should have tended to him hours ago when the fingers of badness might have been expunged more easily and the shaking had not overtaken all sense of ease. With a quick slash of her blade she opened the torn material in his hose from groin to knee. The swollen flesh on his upper thigh had been crushed and she knew instantly that there was nothing more that she could do. Bending to his chest, she listened for the pulse of blood.

'Can you help him?' There was a tone in James's voice she had not heard before.

'Help comes in many forms.' Isobel was careful to take the emotion she felt away from her answer as she dribbled water through cracked and shaking lips, waiting for a moment while he swallowed to give him the chance to savour the wetness. Already she could feel the rattle of death in his chest, reverberating against her arm, a soft portent of an ending that was near. 'My father used to say help was always only fiscal, but my husband insisted it was otherwise. He was a man inclined to the spiritual, you understand, before he died. Your friend here, though, needs another gift entirely and any aid given to another in reaching the afterlife easily has a reward all of its own.'

She saw the quick flicker of rebellion in his leaf-green eyes before he had a chance to hide it, loss entwined amongst anger. Biting down on her own grief, she laid her hand across the dying stranger's throat, feeling the beat, weaker now and more erratic in the last emptying of blood.

He would still hear, she knew, still make sense of a world fading into quiet and she wanted him to understand the music inherent in a land his dust would be for ever a part of.

'The smell of the sea is always close in Fife. We're used to that here, used to living with the wind coming up the Firth funnelled into briskness and calling. The birds call, too, the curlews and the linnets, their song in the birch and the beech and the pine, and further west Benarty guards the heavens and gathers the clouds.'

Her land, its boundaries drawn in blood and fought for in a passion that was endless. The earth here would guard Simon, fold him into her warmth and hold him close. These were the old laws of dying, the rules that had been forgotten in the new kingdom of Scotland because men looked forwards now and never back.

She should be numbed to death, immune to its loss, but she was not and even a stranger who had walked with her for less than a day was mourned.

She had been married once? The thought made him stiffen as he watched her speak of the streams and the mountains and the flowers in springtime. Like a song of the living to the ears of the dying, he was to think later, and a prayer for transport somewhere easier and without pain. Her eyes remained dry.

A gift she had said, and indeed it was that, devoid of angst or panic or alarm. Simon simply slipped off and never moved again as she invoked a pathway to Heaven and talked of a good man that she wanted him to find there named Alisdair.

When death began to cool his flesh she stood, a little off balance. He would have liked to offer her his help, but he was uncertain as to whether she would accept it or not. As they looked at each other, the distance of a few feet felt like the world.

'What was he to you, this Simon?'

'A friend.'

'And the other man, the one you held safe in the sea?'

'Guy. My cousin.'

'Then you are blessed with the love of others.'

The love of others! If only she knew. He stayed silent as Isobel turned Simon towards the ocean.

'Spirits look eastwards for their home.'

'I have not read that in any Bible.' He tried to keep his voice even.

'Some things are not written. They are simply known.' Clearing a path to the sea, she uprooted bracken and small plants to leave an easy access.

He waited till she had finished before reaching forwards to take one of her hands. When he looked down he saw her fingernails were all bitten to the quick and that there was a wedding band on her marriage finger.

'Thank you.'

She did not pull away, but stood still, her eyes this close ringed with a pure and clear gold. He tried not to glance down at the scar she wore so indifferently.

'How long have you been married?'

She broke the contact between them with a single hard jerk. Lord, was nothing ever simple with her? Her hair had escaped the confines of a leather band and the lad's hose had dropped to the line of her hips, and where the short tunic had hitched upwards the gap showed a good expanse of skin.

'How old are you?'

'Twenty-three.'

'You look younger.'

'Do I?' For the first time since meeting Isobel Dalceann, he detected feminine uncertainty and a strange feeling twisted around his heart.

She had rescued him from a raging sea and sewn

his arm up without flinching, yet here when he gave her a compliment she blushed like a young girl. The contradictions in her were astonishing.

'We will wrap your friend in a blanket and leave him undisturbed until help arrives.'

'Help?'

'Angus will bring others.'

'Tonight?'

'Perhaps.' Gathering a handful of sticks from the beach, she placed them in a pile. The scar on her hand in the fall of the eve was easily seen and he wondered again who had hurt her so very badly.

'The keep you mention, is it your family's?'

'Aye, it is that and by virtue of long possession. The Dalceann have ruled the land around Ceann Gronna for centuries.'

'So you hold tenure direct from the Crown?'

Suspicion sparked across her face, changing eyes to deep brown. 'Where exactly did you say you were from?'

'I didn't.'

'But not from Edinburgh?' The brittle anger in her words was palpable.

'No. Burgundy.'

The tinder was set in the small fire and he flinted it, blowing at the flame until it took. Soon there was a blazing roar.

Isobel plucked the birds and threaded them through a stick she had sharpened with her knife.

They were held in place by two piles of stones across the flames, more embers than fire now. She had added other berries he did not recognise, their red skins splitting in the heat. Everything she did showed prowess, competency and a knowledge of the bounty of this land.

'What did you do there in France?'

'Many things.'

'Was soldiering one of them?'

He stayed silent. With no idea of the leanings of the Dalceann cause save the knowledge of an ancient patriarchal title, he needed to be careful. The unrest in Scotland had filtered into France, after all, and David's hold on the country had always been tenuous. Edward the Third of England had his champion in the factions of Edward Balliol and the vagaries of clan law had never existed under simple allegiances.

Besides, his head swam in a way that was alarming and the prickling heat from the flames made him move back into the cool. If he had been stronger, he could have walked away into the night and tracked west along the Firth, but the shaking that had plagued Simon was beginning to plague him, too. Grinding his teeth together, he swallowed and closed his eyes to find balance.

He rarely answered a question, she noticed.

She also noticed the sweat on his brow and the way his cheeks had flushed with heat. It was his wound, no doubt, the badness settling in. She should unwind the cloth and wash the injury over and over with water that was too hot to touch, infused with the garlic she had so carefully stored at Ceann Gronna.

But here in the open, with nothing save that which she had already used, she wondered if it would not be better to leave it till the morrow when they reached the keep.

If she was a proper healer she might have been able to make the call, but warfare had taken up all the years of her life and it was true when Ian had said that she was more skilled in the art of killing.

Still she did have valerian and the special medicine from England to stop him thrashing about and hurting himself. He would be thirsty and the powders were tasteless. Her fingers felt the paper twists in the pocket of her tunic and she held them safe in her palm. James was large so the dose would be high. Not so high as to kill him though, she amended.

She smiled as she saw his gaze upon her.

'I will fetch cold water from the stream before we eat.'

The rain sounded far away. He felt it on his face when he tipped his head, but the sky that it fell from was blurred and hollow, no true sense in any of it.

Isobel Dalceann sat watching him, the meat between them blackening on the stick, overcooked and forgotten. He should have moved forwards and taken it from the flame, but his hand felt odd and heavy, too much weight to bother with.

Closing his eyes, he opened them again, widening the lids in a way that allowed more light.

'How do you feel?'

Her words were flat.

'How should I feel?'

'Tired?'

Understanding dawned. 'You put something in the water?' He made to rise, but his knees buckled under his weight and he fell to the side heavily. She did not blink as she watched him struggle.

'Why?' It was all he could manage, the numbness around his lips making it hard to speak. His tongue felt too big in his mouth.

'Because you are a stranger,' she answered, 'and because everything is dangerous.'

He conserved his breath and closed his eyes. Was the concoction lethal? Already his heart was speeding up and sweat garnered in the cold. He should have been more on guard, he thought and swore at his own stupidity.

'You won't die,' she said flatly, the firelight falling in rough shadows across her eyes. 'It is an opiate of valerian and gentle unless you fight it.'

Such a quiet warning. He almost spoke, but the dark was claiming him, his world spinning into all the corners of quiet.

* * *

She cushioned a blanket beneath his cheek and another across his shoulders. Her fingers she passed beneath his nose, glad when she felt the gentle passage of air. She had not killed him and, unconscious, her prisoner would be so very much easier to protect.

Already she could hear them coming through the trees, the light that she had noticed reflected in the hills above a good few hours ago giving her knowledge of their presence.

Angus would be leading them and he would be looking for vengeance. Please God, that James had told the truth about leaving Ian alive, for if he had not…

She shook her head, repositioning her knife on the inside of her kirtle's sleeve. These days she trusted no one, for David's edict calling on the forfeiture of Dalceann land made everything tenuous. Troublesome vassals needed replacement with more amenable ones, after all, and there were many lining up for the rich largesse that was Ceann Gronna.

Even this one, perhaps? Her eyes went to James's face.

He looked so much softer in sleep than in wakefulness. His nose had been broken somewhere in the past, the fine white line on the ridge leaving a bump to one side. His clothes still worried her, for the velvet surcoat was finely stitched, every seam doubled into dark green ribbon and his bliaud was of fashionable cotton. For the first time she saw a scar just above the fleshy cushion of his palm, dangerously close to the blue lines of blood at his wrist.

No small wound that. She imagined how it must have bled out and the effort it would have taken to quell such a flow. It looked deliberately done, too. Like the mark of a sacrifice.

But there were voices now, only a few hundred yards away. Positioning herself before him, she watched the track from where her clansmen would come, on the other side of the clearing.

Andrew came first, followed by Angus. Both looked for Ian.

'Your brother is back in the glade where I left you, Angus,' she said.

'He hurt him. The one from the sea. He kicked out with his hands tied and brought him down. If he has killed him...'

'He says he did not.'

As his glance flicked across to James, Angus pushed forward, intent written in every line of his face.

'No.' Isobel held the knife where he could see it and he stopped.

'I am a Dalceann...'

'And he is asleep.'

'Drugged?' Andrew spoke, his voice imbued with the quiet knowledge of something being not quite as it ought.

'Aye. The wound ails him. I stitched it and cleaned it, but it still bleeds.'

'And the other?'

'He died a few hours back. The cold of the sea sat inside him like ice.'

A dozen Ceann Gronna soldiers shuffled into the clearing as they spoke and Isobel tipped her head at their coming, their full-length mantles folded against the chill.

'I want this stranger unhurt. We will send him by boat to Edinburgh with the ferrymen from the landing-place and he will be no further nuisance.'

'Nae.' Angus paced across the other side of the fire. 'He is not one of us. I say kill him here and now and be rid of any menace.'

In response Isobel kneeled beside James. Pushing back her sleeve, she made a cut in her palm and another across the thickened skin below the strange mark on his wrist. Pressing them together, she smelt the rusty tang of blood.

Hecate, Cerridwen, Dark Mother Take Us In
Hecate, Cerridwen, Let Us Be Reborn.

The oath of loyalty and attachment echoed around the clearing.

'You would protect him for ever?' Andrew asked the question.

She shook her head, knowing he was her enemy. 'Nae. But I swear by all the gods of this place that I will protect him for now.'

Chapter Four

He was naked.

He knew that as easily as he knew he was safe.

Isobel Dalceann was there in the shadow just beyond the candlelight, watching him with her dark eyes and stillness.

'Water.' He could barely get the word out.

She moved forwards and he saw that one eye was swollen, the deep bruise on her cheek below grazed into redness.

'Who hurt you?' His whisper was barely audible as she leaned forwards to hear.

'I fell.'

He did not believe it, nor did he understand the shift of caution in her eyes or the gentle way she took a cloth and ran it across his chest.

'It feels good.' All the skin on his arms was raised with pleasure, leaning into the cool, and he saw she had a band of cloth wrapped around her palm. Another hurt. He tried to reach up and touch it, but she stopped him.

'You must rest. Your arm has festered and only strength can save you now.'

His arm? Sliced in the sea. He remembered the boat bound for Edinburgh. He remembered the wave as it had caught them broadside, turning the vessel into the cold and green, the ropes tethering him and the sailcloth, people calling from everywhere.

He had cut free as many as he could with his knife and released them. Simon. Guy. Etienne and Raoul. Then the wooden splint had come down from the mast, broken by force of wind and wave above, turning sharp.

Aching now. Right down to his fingers in a cramping stiffness. A band circled his arm, white linen soaked in something that smelt like overripe onion and herbs strangely mixed. He could not move a muscle.

'My sword hand?'

'Ian says cloth sellers should have no need for such a weapon,' she returned.

'You found him, then, in the glade?'

'Worse for wear with the knots you fashioned. It would have been a slow death had we come too late.'

'Like this one is?'

Her pupils dilated. Always a sign of high emotion. Marc shut his eyes. She thought that he would die soon. Tonight even, he amended, looking at the ornate golden cross above his bed.

Other words came close. An ancient chant in the firelight! Isobel Dalceann lifting his palm against her own and cutting it open, blood mixed in an oath of protection. Was he going mad as well?

The glow from the candle hurt even though his eyelids burnt in fever.

'Where am I?'

'Ceann Gronna. My keep on the high sea cliffs above Elie.'

The sea was close, the moon seen through the space between skin and stone at the window. No longer full.

'How long?'

'Three days.'

He breathed out, nausea roiling his stomach. Even in Burgundy when the arrow had pierced his armour and gone deep into his back he had not been as ill.

'You have tended me, then?'

Sickness. The room was full of its grasp. Basins, cloths and vials of medicine lined up on the table. His clothes were neatly washed and folded on the seat of a white ash wooden chair decorated with bands of vermilion paint. He wished he might have stood and taken charge, but not one muscle in his body would obey a command.

Helpless. The very word stung with shock.

'You have spoken in your sleep in French of battles and of death. It is just as well that none here understand you.'

He turned then, away from her eyes, because there was a question in them that he had no answer for.

Are you an enemy?

Once I was, he wanted to say, but now? The bruising on her cheek was dark.

He should have kept silent, should have held his tongue even in the grasp of delirium. So many damn secrets inside him.

'When you are better, you will be sent by boat across to Edinburgh.'

'Better?' The word surprised him. She thought he would survive this, then, this malady. Relief had him reaching out and taking her fingers into his own. Just gratitude in it. The cool of her skin made him realise how hot he was.

Isobel stood still, the nighttime noises of a sleeping keep far from this room. Her room. His fingers were strong like his body, the skin on the pads toughened by work. She felt them relax as he fell into sleep again, but she did not put his hand down as she should have, did not move from her position at his side, watching him in the midnight.

Marc. He had said his name was that when she had called him James, shrugging off the other name with agitation. He had said other things as well in his delusion that had made her glad she was alone, his green eyes glassy with the fever that raged through him, taking sense.

A warrior. She understood that now by all the other marks on his body, sliced into history. Neither an easy life nor a safe one, for fire and shadow sculptured the hardness in him lying on her bed.

He had spoken of some things that she had no knowledge of and of other things that she did.

Things such as the sovereignty accorded to David of the Scots and the ambitions of Philip of France. A king's man, then? If Ian or Andrew had heard the words he would be long gone by now, breathless in the raging seas off the end of the Ceann Gronna battlements, only memory.

Why did she protect him?

Her eyes travelled over his body, masculine and beautiful, and with real regret she covered the shape with a thin linen cloth. Wiping back her hair with the sudden heat, she felt the raised ridge of scar and frowned.

Broken apart. By trust. It would never happen again.

With a ripe expletive she turned from the sleeping stranger and walked to the window to watch the water silver in the Scottish moonlight.

The knock on the door a few moments later pulled her from her thoughts. Andrew stood there, a pewter mug of ale in one hand and the remains of a crust of bread in the other. He walked over to Marc and laid a finger against his throat, before coming back to the doorway.

'He is still out, I see. Ye'll be needing help I'm thinking, lass. This captive is a way from healthy and the rings beneath your eyes are dark.'

Shaking off his concern, she faced him. 'He is making progress, none the less. A day or two and he will be fit to travel.'

'To Edinburgh, then. Is that wise?'

'He has not seen the keep or the structures within it. Nor will he be given knowledge of the tunnels or of the entrance from the sea. He knows only this room,' she added. 'We will blindfold him when he leaves so that nothing is seen.'

'Something is always seen, Isobel, and he looks like no cloth merchant I have ever encountered.' The frown on his brow was deep. Concern for the security of the Ceann Gronna Castle, Isobel supposed, and those within it. A just concern, too, and yet...

'If we kill him in cold blood we are as bad as those who come to oust us.'

Andrew laughed. 'When David sends the next baron this summer to try his hand at the sacking of the keep, you might think differently.'

'So you would have him as dead as Ian wants him?'

'Not dead, but gone. The day after tomorrow even if he is no better. Do ye promise me that?'

The cut on her palm stung when she shook his

hand and her right cheek ached from where Angus had hit out in the clearing after she had invoked the protections.

Probably warranted, she thought. She didn't recognise herself in the action, either, as for so many years any stranger trespassing on the Dalceann lands had been sent away without exception.

Why not him?

Why not bundle him right now into a blanket and dispatch him west? He could take his chances of survival just as the others had taken theirs, and if God saw fit to let him live then who was she to invite danger to her hearth?

The Ceann Gronna hearth. She remembered when as a little girl her father had remodelled the fireplace in the solar, burying iron beneath the stones for preservation.

Lord, and then her father's actions had inveigled them all into this mess when he had stood against the king in Edinburgh and demanded that the lands around this place would be for ever Dalceann. He had taken no notice of any arguments Alisdair had put forward, but had forged on into a position which he was caught in. The armies that had followed him home had been undermanned and he had easily rebuffed them, but by then they were outlawed. Surrender would undoubtedly mean death to them all and Isobel had long been one to whom strategy had come easily.

At twenty she had planned the defence of the next attack and the one after that. Now, they stood on the edge of the cliff with the world at a distance and no other great vassal of the king had ventured forth to try his hand at possession. Not for two whole summers.

So far the magic in the hearth had held. Except for Alisdair. But even his bones lay here in the earth of the bailey, defended by high walls of stone.

The unassailable Ceann Gronna Castle of the Dalceann clan.

'We cannae hold on for ever, ye ken, Isobel. The new governance has its supporters.'

She nodded because truth was an unavoidable thing. When the time was right some of the Dalceanns would leave the keep by sea. Already the ground to the south was prepared. A different ruse and one bought with the golden trinkets and jewellery found in the French boat that had sunk a good two years before. There was still some left in case of trouble, hidden in the walls of her chamber. Alisdair's idea.

'If this stranger is as inclined to violence as Ian believes him to be, it would make sense to bind him in the dungeon under lock and key.'

'You speak as if I could not subdue him, Andrew, should he become restless.'

'Could not or would not, Isobel? There is a difference.'

His voice held a note of question and it saddened her. He had always been the father her own had not been—a man of strong morals and good sense.

A moan behind had her turning.

'I will think on your words, Andrew, I promise.'

She was glad when he merely nodded and moved off, leaving her alone to tend to the green-eyed stranger.

She had said something of sea tunnels, Marc thought, and of an entrance from the water, but with Isobel beside him again, her hand across his brow, cooling fever, he filed the information away to remember at a later time.

His arm ached, small prickles of it in his chest and neck, the water she helped him sip tainted with a herb he did not know the name of.

The door held a key in the lock and there was rope in the shelf of a small cabinet. A fine woollen cloth hung on the wall by the bed. All things he could use to escape if he needed to he thought. But not yet. The weakness in him was all consuming and the dizziness took away his balance.

'You need to get stronger,' she said and her tone was angry. 'For my protection has its limits, *Marc.*'

Marc felt his lips tug up at each end. Not in humour, but in the sheer and utter absurdity of it all. God, when had he ever depended on anyone before and how many thousands had always depended on him? She had the way of his name, too. The fever, he supposed, loosening his tongue in the heat of swelter.

'They would kill me here? Your people?'

She nodded. 'For a lot less than you would imagine.'

'And you? Are you compromised because of it?'

When she did not answer he swore, the night in the forest coming back to him. Lifting his right hand, he motioned to the wound.

'Your blood and mine?'

'The spirit of guardianship must be honoured in the proper way. It is written.'

'A useful knowledge, that.'

'You speak as if you do not believe it.'

'Believe?' Turmoil and battle were all he had known for a long time now. But Isobel smelt of fresh mint and soap and something else he could not as yet name. He closed his eyes so that he might know it better, every sense focusing on the part of his skin where her hair brushed against him, soft as a feather.

Hope!

The word came down with all the force of a heavy-bladed falchion—he who had led armies for the king against the great enemies of France for all the years of his life. Trusting no one. Guarding any careless faith.

It was the sickness, perhaps, that made him vulnerable or the mix of her blood against his own, inviting exposure.

He wondered just what she would do if she knew who he truly was and pressed down the thought.

Just now and just here. A room in a keep above the sea, its buttressed walls holding in a danger that it had long tried to keep without. He closed his eyes to stop her from seeing what he knew lay inside him, fermenting in the deceit, and was glad when she left the room.

She had seen the look in his eyes and needed to think. Seen the danger and the menace and the hidden knowledge of threat. Not to her though, she thought, as she went down the stairs, the heat of his fever imbued into the very tissue of her skin. She had locked the door and taken the key to keep the others out.

Safety again. For him.

Turning the silver band on her finger, she remembered the man who had put it there. Gentle. Manageable. Alisdair had railed against her father's strong denial of David's right in managing his kingdom and had warned him of the pathway fraught with danger that he would tread should he demand authority of the Dalceann tracts.

All his warnings had come to pass, save the one of losing his own life while in the process of trying to change her father's mind.

She swore beneath her breath. 'Listen to your heart, Isobel,' her husband had said time and time again as they had lain in their curtained bed above the storms thrown in from the churning German Sea. 'King David's Norman education is changing everything in Scotland and only those who can change with it will survive.'

Slapping one hand against her thigh, she leaned back against a wall. Solid and cool, it steadied her.

Alone.

God in Heaven, why should such aloneness today be any worse than usual?

It was because of this outlander.

It all came down to him. His skin beneath her fingers as she wiped his brow. His breath against her face when she leaned in close, eyes of deep clear green shored up by carefulness.

His body marked by war and battle. She had told no one that!

Neither had she disclosed the silver ring she had found buried deep in the pocket of his gilded surcoat and engraved with the royal mark of King David.

Another day and she would have him gone. She swore it on the soul of Brighid, the Celtic Goddess, the keeper of the sacred hearth and the patroness of women.

Isobel Dalceann came back to him as the sun fell low against the window and she brought a mash of sorts with bread soaked in milk. He ate it as if it was his very last meal and felt stronger.

'Thank you.'

Again. It seemed of late he had been indebted to this woman time after time.

Waving away the words, she countered with her own question. 'Are you one of David's men?'

She had found the ring, he supposed. He should have tossed it when he had the chance, but the piece held a value to him that was sentimental and he had not wanted to.

'Once I was,' he replied.

'And now?'

'It has been a while since I was in his company.'

She moved back and he knew he had erred.

'You knew him, then, personally.'

The furrow on her brow deepened. Thinking. He could almost see her brain turn.

'My mother was from the House of Valois in Burgundy. David of Scotland gave me the ring when he lived there.'

'Under the protection of Philip the Sixth?'

So she knew her politics. He nodded.

'You are a friend of the king's, then?' The words fell into the silence of the room, the talk marking him off as…what?

When she breathed out heavily he knew she had not wanted this truth. A simple soldier or sailor would have been so very much easier to deal with. Still, in the face of all her assistance he found it difficult to lie.

'Many here at Ceann Gronna have already died under the guise of David's ambitions.' Her voice was flat and hard.

'And I can promise you that I should not wish to bring one other person here harm.'

She swore again at that, a ripe curse that was better suited to a man. The lad's hose were tight against the rise of her bottom and despite his sickness he felt his body react.

'If I was braver, I would slit your throat as surely as you wanted to slit Ian's.'

'What stops you, then?'

'This,' she answered and leant down into him, her mouth running across his lips. Not gently, either, but with a full carnal want that left him reeling. He felt her bite his bottom lip before her tongue probed, felt the sharp slant of desire and the fierce pull of lust. Felt her fingers on his face and throat and then on his nipples pinching, the rush of hunger acute. When she had finished she moved back, wiping the taste of him away with the top of her uninjured hand.

'There is not much to hinder the path of a woman taking a man.' Her eyes went to the stiff hardness that was so very easily seen through the thin linen cloth covering him.

'Men hold to the premise of self-satisfaction far more than any woman is likely to, you see. A small caress here, a whisper there, the cradling of flesh between clever fingers...'

Hell, she was a witch. He looked away because every single thing she said was true and because the need to come right then and there before her was overriding.

He had not kissed her back. The knowledge of it ran into her veins and made her step away, his face dim in the shadow. If a man had taken liberties like that with her, she might have killed him, quickly, with the knife she always kept in the leather holder under the sleeve of her kirtle.

But he seemed at home in silence as he waited for her to speak, his palms opened on the bed beside him as if the matter had not compromised him in the very least.

Perhaps it is the mix of our blood that has tainted me, she thought, as he began to speak.

'How long ago did your husband die?'

'Two years ago in the coming spring.'

'Have you lain with another since?'

The question shocked her because she had counted her many months of celibacy every night since the sea storm.

The very thought of it made her ashamed. A woman who might sacrifice everything for the quick tug of lust. And she knew what obligations kept her here, above the water watching out for her enemies.

She had not forgotten the promise made to her husband the day he had died, the day she had tried to take her father's arrow from him, embedded in his body.

'You shall always have my heart, Isobel,' Alisdair had said, as the blood filled his mouth in bubbles. 'So could I take yours with me?'

In death he had meant. In the last breaths of thought.

She had laid his hands across her breast above the beat of loss, his fingers long and slender and soft. She could still feel them there sometimes as life had left him, tugging against the ebb of death.

Twenty-one and abandoned to any other hope of passion because those clansmen gathered about her dying husband had all heard his plea and her whispered answer.

'Yes,' she had said through the ache of sorrow, every day and every moment she had spent with him imbued in that answer. Until now when another power had turned her, the longing of lust snaking inside deadness. She was glad for the hard measure of this stranger's cock beneath the cover because at least some part of his body had wanted her in the same way that she had wanted him.

It still stood proud and he made no move to hide it, lying there like an offering he had no mind to give.

'If I left my seed in you and it took, I cannot think that you would be safe here.'

Reason and logic, she thought savagely as she shook her head, wanting something else entirely. Her husband Alisdair had been the very master of such emotions, and sometimes all she had longed for was wild abandon.

Chapter Five

He was dressed when Isobel went in to her sleeping chamber the next morning, sitting to one side of the bed and watching the door.

In the light of the day her advances of the previous day seemed ill-advised and inappropriate. She also felt tired and scratchy from a night spent in a cot off the solar, reliving her mistake, sleep eluding her as an unwanted excitement crept into possibility.

Lord, Alisdair's kisses had never stirred such inescapable power, remaining only tepid versions of those from a man who hadn't even kissed her back. The blood ran into her cheeks like a force and she hated the reaction, a shallow irrational nonsense more suited to the constitution of a vapid courtly maiden. Straightening, she schooled her face back into indifference.

'You look better today.'

He smiled, the lines around his eyes deepening.

'Is it recorded anywhere, my lady, that a kiss is the most potent of all medicines?'

His clemency in the face of her breach in manners was welcomed.

'Andrew came to see you this morning?'

'Indeed. He felt a further day here might be over-extending my welcome.'

'He is a good man...' She went to say more, but he held up his hand.

'A good man who is frightened. Everyone here is. I can feel it when you speak of the Dalceann land and its claimants.'

Her laugh was false, high and shallow. 'A man newly arrived from Burgundy can hardly wish to be embroiled in our sorry state of affairs.'

This would be the last conversation between them! She did not want him to leave on the promise of something he would come to regret when he arrived in Edinburgh. Another hour and he would be gone. Smiling probably, when he reached the city in the company of his friends and told them about a woman who had kissed him unbidden, a fierce woman with a badly scarred face and wearing simple lad's clothing.

Yet still she could not abandon him.

Taking his knife from the basket, she handed it over, watching as he placed it in the folds of the velvet surcoat at the end of the bed. Only a small pile of possessions rescued from the sea. 'I have sharpened and honed it myself. If you would conceal it so that no others see, I would be grateful.'

He stood as she spoke, his tallness surprising her yet again, for it was seldom that men towered above her.

'God's blood, Isobel.' It was the first time he had used her name, the sound of it skewered into prettiness by his accent. She swallowed as he took her hand, running his forefinger across the cut on her palm so very gently.

'You are like a caged bird here at Ceann Gronna, beautiful of feather but clipped of wing. Come with me to Edinburgh and plead the cause of the Dalceann keep in my company.'

Her heart raced. 'Nae, it is not possible.'

She thought of David's anger at the Dalceann intransigence and the men he had sent to marry her when he perceived the vacuum of power to be dangerous to the defence of his own realm after Alisdair had died. The barons and magnates who had strode into Fife later, on the command of their king, only coveted Ceann Gronna Castle as they sought a loveless and compromised betrothal with its chieftain.

'I would ask of you a favour, though. There is a blindfold in the basket. Would you wear it without argument when Andrew and his men come for you?'

'To keep the secrets of this place intact?'

She could only nod her head as he asked and hope that it was not his death warrant she was signing and that Andrew would hold to his promise of a safe passage.

'If I say yes, could I petition something from you, too?' His words were soft as their eyes met and she could not look away.

'Could you kiss me again?'

She turned, thinking he was making fun of her, a joke against the morning bathed in harsh light, the disfigurement on her face so very easily seen. But he caught her, gentle in his strength, the white of his tunic against the darkness of skin. Closer with warmth, as his mouth came to hers, no hesitation in it.

He kissed like a warrior would, taking what he needed without discourse to the properness of society, her timid answer pushed away into sheer and blazing want. It ran in white-hot shards to her stomach and her loins like an old knowledge. Alisdair had been a gentle man and her childhood sweetheart, his ardour limited by reason, logic and a certain reserve. Marc kissed her with a hint of the nobleman ransacked by the sheer power of a fighting knight, his mouth slanting down to her throat and the skin below that, and then turning his tongue to her breast.

She could not push away, or call a halt. All she wanted was more, her head tilted, eyes glassed with surrender, the feel of his muscle beneath her fingers, honed by time and battle.

Digging in her nails, she felt him flinch, but she wanted to mark him before he left, wanted him to remember that he had kissed her with her full desire, layered under all the reasons of why she should not have.

As he finished he held her face against his chest, the beat of his heart wildly quick, her hope rising with such lack of control.

She wanted to say, stay for ever, in her arms, in this keep, in this one room and well away from the communion of others. She wanted to tell him that under the scars and the boy's clothes a woman lay who had long been bereft of the ministrations of a virile male. She wanted to cry as she had when she was a young maid, weeping at the very unfairness of her life, lost in politics and greed and war, rent from this to that by the pretensions of parents who held no care for her welfare.

But to say all that disregarded her history as a Dalceann and her love for Andrew and Ian and Angus and the many other men and women who had stood with her against the wrath of both her father and a long-absent monarch.

So in the end she said nothing because it was easier to do so and because it would lead him safely away from Ceann Gronna and the siege in the coming spring.

Another summer and it would be over.

David had lost patience with a little force and was amassing a bigger one. She had heard rumours from passing bards who criss-crossed the provinces of Fife, Strathearn and Menteith, singing for their supper.

She thought then that she did not even know her

green-eyed stranger's proper name, a man tossed into her life by an angry sea and then tossed out of it again by the shifting will of monarchs.

But her time had run out, for Andrew was coming up the stairs. She knew his step against the stone, his men behind him. Breaking away, she stood on the other side of the room as they entered.

'Morag is looking for you in the kitchen, Isobel. I said I would send ye down when I saw you.'

She knew what he was doing, giving her an excuse to leave the room before Marc was blindfolded and taken. She saw the rope in Andrew's hands and the knife at his belt, sharp enough to cut into a man's throat like butter. Swallowing, she shook her head and stayed still.

'We can do this gentle or you can make it hard,' Andrew said, turning to the one he had come for. 'But ye will be on that ferry for Edinburgh come the morrow, I swear it either way.'

'As long as I am still alive,' Marc returned. 'Does Ian accompany us?'

'No. It's difficult enough to traverse the countryside without watching for revenge.'

'Thank you.'

Marc shrugged on his surcoat, the red velvet looking a little perished under the laundering it had suffered from an over-enthusiastic washing maid, the braid on one shoulder drooping. The knife was nowhere at all to be seen and Isobel was astonished by

Marc's sleight of hand for she knew it must be there. A small comfort that, if his wrists were to be tied.

Taking the blindfold from her basket, she held it out, watching as he took it and placed it against his eyes before Andrew checked it.

He would not see her again!

The thought came to Isobel in a piercing ache, but she stayed still as they led him from the room, his hand held against Andrew's arm for direction. He did not look back or hesitate.

At the first-floor landing window she waited as they came through the door on the ground floor, more men with them now, their voices reaching her from the distance.

He fell even as she turned to leave, the foot of one of the Dalceann soldiers coming between his legs. With bound hands he could not cushion his fall, his head cracking against the coping stones on the side of the pathway.

As he was roughly gathered back upright Isobel swore, for even at this distance she saw the blindfold had been lifted and that the secrets of Ceann Gronna, so carefully kept, had been compromised.

Andrew in his usual fashion of quick thinking pulled it back down, shielding the others from such notice. Marc's blood ran down his hands.

Her options narrowed. If she ran out as one who might heal the wound, would he be safer? Or in more danger? Would Andrew cut his losses and call in death as the certain way to still a wagging tongue despite her earlier heartfelt pleadings? Already she could see Ian circling to one side of the group.

Without breath she counted.

One.

Two.

Three.

Seconds that he was not dead. The soldiers began again to walk and Marc did not falter, his fingers again at the crook of Andrew's arm, and his lips moving as though he spoke. What did he say? she wondered, as Andrew's hand stole to the hilt of the knife at his belt.

Undercurrents. Refuge and danger mixed in the face of desperate men who shepherded an enemy towards the inner wall. Once through the barbican he would be lost from view, the horses waiting in the outer bailey. Taking in breath, she held it and felt pain wind its way in a heavy ache right down to the pit of her stomach.

He still lived! Lord in Heaven, he had expected a knife through his ribs long before he felt the wind from the outside world on his face or the smell of horse flesh in his nostrils. Andrew's influence probably. When he had gone down against the stone he had not expected to get up again, but then neither had he envisaged seeing the secrets of the layout of the Dalceann keep.

Even the castles in France had not been as secure with their defensive merlons and crenels and thick round concentric walls. Admiration clambered over pain.

He was bleeding badly. His tongue felt the damage to his lip, a soft mass of flesh hanging to one side.

When the portcullis shut behind them, iron chains jangling with the effort, Andrew removed the blindfold and the light flooded in where darkness lingered, hurting his eyes. He squinted against the brightness.

'We will clean ye up when we get to the valley stream. As it is, you look like you have been in a week-long stramash.'

Marc didn't speak, his mind taking in all the undulations of the land before the castle. Pits and holes and ditches. For the first time he saw just how close the sea was, cliffs caught at the very edge of the outer wall, and falling to rocks below.

The Firth entrance Isobel had spoken of when she had presumed him unconscious would be there somewhere, too, probably within the small promontory of land jutting from the middle.

Unassailable!

Unless you had some inside knowledge of the place. Perceiving interest from Andrew, he turned and smiled.

'I was lucky to survive such a sea.' Any topic to deflect his interest in the fortifications of Ceann Gronna!

'Here are the horses.' His captor's voice held only the frustration of a long ride and Marc was relieved to have been given his own steed so that he was not forced to share the saddle with another.

He wondered what sort of a rider Isobel Dalceann was, shaking away the answer with his own impatience.

She was probably as gifted at the art of horsemanship as she was at swimming.

And kissing!

'Lord above,' he muttered as Andrew cut his bindings with a verbal warning to behave. Hoisting himself on his mount, he threaded the reins through his numb-sore hands so that he would maintain his seat even in a gallop.

Isobel held the ring with the silver marks of David the Second in her palm, the stamp of the smithies who had fashioned the piece written in the smooth inside circle.

Everything the stranger had had on his person was of inordinate value: his clothes, the braided bracelet, the jewel-encrusted dagger and this bauble, with its official royal standard burnished by time.

'Enough!' Her voice pierced the silence around her, echoing in the stone as she moved her chest a foot from its normal standing place.

Carefully she pushed in the flagstone behind it and watched it turn on an axis. The few pieces of dust and mortar that fell she wiped up with a wet cloth from the ewer, remembering her husband's insistence that she always do so.

Behind in the cavity the gold lay, bands of jewels and sturdy goblets stacked on leather.

The French gold with two coins that she had never seen there before balanced on the top!

Fear rose quickly as she perceived the unexpected breach of security. She should never have opened it with someone else in the room, even if she had thought him unconscious at the time. Swearing beneath her breath at the ease in which her safe-keeping had been violated, she looked inside.

What was missing? Sorting through the treasure she saw none was gone and that it had only been added to. Lifting the silver coins, she read the inscriptions in French.

Marc. What else had he known? She remembered the blindfold falling askew when he had tripped and her words with Andrew when she thought him to be unconscious. Perhaps he had over-listened?

She had spoken of the sea entrance and of the sacking of Ceann Gronna.

Clever. Too clever. A man of two kings and the scars of many battles to prove it.

Her finger traced the outline of her lips and she swore. Had he distracted her purposefully with such a sensual assault and had she just let the serpent out of Eden?

Chapter Six

'If you should want for warmth tonight, Marc, my rooms are only a moment or so from your own.'

The promise in the eyes of the sensual Duchess of Kinburn made him step back.

'I do not have the inclination to kill your husband should he find out where you have strayed, Lady Anne,' he said, prying her fingers loose from the fabric of his sleeve. 'And neither do I have the time. Our king is waiting to speak with me in his chamber.'

'Ahh, but you have been here in Edinburgh for all of a month, my lord, and alone at nights by the numerous accounts I have heard. Surely there is one woman here who would take your fancy?' She leaned into him so that the front of her bejewelled kirtle fell low on the line of her generous bosom, her flaxen hair tumbling across alabaster skin.

Beautiful, Marc mused, but the idea of bedding her did not raise his appetite even a little. The thought concerned him as he turned, striding through the antechambers of the king with purpose.

A month since he had arrived here from the Queen's Landing ferry. A month since he had seen Isobel Dalceann with terror in her eyes as she had given him the blindfold, her hands shaking with the effort of it.

Marc had kept quiet about his time in the Ceann Gronna keep because in the labyrinth that was politics in Scotland he had discovered the lengths David was prepared to go to in order to quell the barons who would not swear allegiance to the Crown.

As the Dalceann clan had not.

He had only been in the Scottish Court for one hour before he first heard the name of the reviled chatelaine of Ceann Gronna mentioned.

'Unmarriageable Isobel with the ugly scarred face.' He wondered how close the person who had circulated this rumour could have got to her, because once you saw the gold in her eyes you understood the depth of everything else that she was and her disfigurement paled into insignificance.

Lord, the anger in him hummed at such vacuousness and he ran his finger down the raised line of flesh on the inside palm of his right hand. An oath of protection given in blood played two ways and he could feel the ghost of her here walking down the corridors of power and laughing. At him and at them, the wind off the sea to her back, lifting her hair into life.

God. She was more real to him in memory than the numerous women at court pushing themselves upon his notice and it worried him.

'Sir Marc.' King David sat before him on a chair decorated in gold embroidery. In his hand he held a document that curled down to his lap, scrawled with fine penmanship.

Beside him the Earl of Huntworth and the Lord of Glencoe hovered, both sipping at wine from expensive silver-stained glassware. When he was handed one similar by a passing servant, he knew the liquid to be Rhenish and very fine.

'Sire.' His bow was deep. Kings had their own brand of arrogance, after all, and he had had plenty of practice in knowing that even one who intimated they were a friend needed careful management.

'I was just telling Glencoe and Huntworth that Feudal Law and Patriarchal Law have their own cause of friction.'

'As double allegiances are often apt to,' Marc replied, the rival ownership of land a constant source of conversation amongst a court bent on the rights of a God-ordained king. A worm of worry turned inside him as the Dalceann charter of sovereignty came to mind. Edinburgh had been abuzz with the topic of Isobel Dalceann and her keep since his arrival. The woman was a witch and a sorceress according to some and the taker of men's minds and will according to others. He had heard of the campaigns mounted against her and of the ineffective sieges laid.

The work of the Underlord, it was whispered, when yet another commander returned home empty handed and broken spirited. Lady Dalceann was in league with the Underworld and with the Forces of Darkness. She had already buried one husband, after all, and it was well known that her father had never been sane. A hag and a hex. An occultist and a necromancer who gained her power from Satan himself. Some said it was the Devil who had marked her in the dead of night, his nails scratching ownership into her cheek as she slept dreaming of him. She wore one of his teeth around her neck, too, it was stated, yellowed with age. Others had told him it was her talisman and her power and if it could be removed nothing of her earthly body would remain. Like smoke, it would disappear back to the realms that had spawned her.

Such information Marc stored, as the woman who had swum through a raging sea at the height of a storm to save lost travellers became explained through the eyes of others.

Dislocated by such wrath and superstition, no wonder Isobel Dalceann was wary and alone. He had said nothing of her to the king.

Lies and secrets.

In Burgundy he had been brought up on such falsity so the hiding of such an omission was not difficult. He could hardly remember a time when he had showed an emotion to another that he had not wished to. He caught his face sometimes in the mirror in passing, a mask of what might be expected from him and reflecting back only that which was expedient and pragmatic. As a youth he had long practised the difficult knack of placing humour both on his lips and in his eyes at will.

His grip tightened around the fragile glass just to the point of breakage. Control again. Seamless and easy.

'They must be taught a lesson, of course. Forfeiture is the penalty for such rife disobedience.' David's face took on the hue of a monarch in high dudgeon.

'And death,' Archibald McQuarry said, the taste of revenge darkening his reply.

Marc had heard that the Earl of Huntworth's\ brother had died in the siege of Ceann Gronna two summers prior and realised that there was more at stake than just the enforcement of law.

He placed his drink carefully down on the nearest table.

'You speak of the Dalceann clan, I presume?' His voice sounded exactly as he wanted it to.

'Indeed we do,' the king replied. 'The vassals of Ceann Gronna keep cannot be left to their own devices, for the northern barons are restless in their own quests. Any sense of uncertainty or loss of monarchical power here in Edinburgh might incite them to better enforce their own positions.'

Checks and balances. In the Scottish court of David the Second and in the French court of Philip the Sixth, power had a way of dividing some men almost as certainly as it had of uniting others.

Greed, hunger and want.

The universals of the honourable knight? Sometimes Marc thought that it was easy, after all, to allow humour into one's eyes.

The deep scar on his back ached with the pain of war and the wound still healing on his arm prickled.

A new battle and this time with the name of a weak and desperate monarch at stake. David would make certain that he did not lose and the Dalceann keep would be sacked as a reminder to others of the dangers inherent in any flagrant disobedience to the Crown.

Even the natural contours of Ceann Gronna's defence would not save it. The trebuchet and mangonels would be numerous in a mission that the Scottish Crown could ill afford to fail at.

'You will leave in the spring with a contingency of two hundred men. You will lead the army, de Courtenay, and these two shall be your commanders. This is what I wish.'

The sour face of Huntsworth told him that the plan was far from the earl's liking.

'Indeed.' Marc raised his glass to such a venture. 'To victory, then,' he toasted.

'And to the end of the Dalceann witch and her lawless followers,' McQuarry added.

Emptying his glass, Marc smiled.

She stood on the high battlement and looked out. Across the water, the silver of the Firth was calm today.

Almost spring. Already the rowan trees around the chapel door budded, and the birches with their lamb's-tail catkins were light against bared bark.

Another few weeks and they would be here. David's men. Two hundred of them if the truth of rumour was proved right, the king's best commanders at their head.

Isobel gritted her teeth so hard that pain shot into the deeper part of her jaw.

Yet Ceann Gronna held its secrets, too, and the preparations for battle had been lengthy and exhaustive. The water supply could never be poisoned, as it ran from far underground, and because of the sea the castle should escape being surrounded. But there were other weaker points that a strong leader might notice. A belfry would allow attackers to make a direct assault on the battlements and the moat could be easily drained with its downward slope.

Even the sea might work against her if any were to guess of the tunnels.

Marc!

It was all her fault that he could even know of them. Had he told? Would he be cognisant of any such plan of siege? Was he still in Scotland or had he left again for his home with Philip the Sixth in Burgundy?

Below her the cries of children reached up, happy in their games with ball and stick. Their mothers would be behind them somewhere, watching, the swell of their stomachs alluding to other Dalceann children needing the care that their name afforded them.

Her care.

Isobel Dalceann. A leader of the Dalceann clan now that her husband had gone and until another could be found to suit.

Marc. Again his name came against her will, crawling into memory. She stamped down on the turn of lust blossoming inside her, tightening her nipples in the wind.

'*Merci aux saints.*' The words were satisfying and she raised one hand before her to feel the cold of the breeze run across her splayed fingers.

Winter had protected them, but it would soon be gone, and in its place danger lurked in the warmth of the longer days.

They would come. She had known that they would come from the south coast to cross the Firth at Queensferry. From there they would strike east towards Largo to Drumeldrie and Kalconquhar to come down into Ceann Gronna standing proud on the promontory before the road wound its way to the sea. And nobody would come to their aid.

Nobody!

They were outcast by the fear of a rampant Crown and an ill-advised disobedience. Her father had been hot tempered and unwise and for years those who peopled the keep had been paying the price of his impolitic judgements. They could not alter it now, for the dissension had gone too far to hope for a mere reprimand and to a certain extent that was her fault, too.

Two years ago when her father and Alisdair had died she might have changed it, might have swayed a clan tired of penalty to raise the flag and surrender, but ruin brought with it a resilience that refused the liability of forfeiture.

All or nothing, her soldiers had roared when the choice had been put to a test and hands had been raised in compliance.

All or nothing.

She was caught.

By winter there would be nothing left, she was sure of it.

Cradling the coin on a chain at her throat, the silver warmed. His coin. Hidden. Concealed. She had worn it like this since he had left, instructing the smithy to run a hole through the middle. Often she felt it, her fingers touching the words and the numbers and the etching of a king on horseback that was not her own.

'Help!' She whispered the word and then added others. 'Please help me.'

A useless entreaty, but appeasing, her heart aching with all that she could not be, for her clan, for her castle, for the history of the Dalceann name that had inhabited this land since the very beginning of time.

The anger in her was such that she trembled with it.

Her name on the wind had her turning and she watched as Andrew came towards her, his hat jammed down across thinning hair and a bandage thick around his wrist.

'Angus said that ye would be here watching. He gave me this to bring you for warmth.'

Passing over a woollen blanket, he waited as she wrapped it about her shoulders.

'Much more of this weather and the Forth will be crossable even for the big war machines.' She met his dark eyes without flinching, hating the message that was plain in what she said.

'Cristina, Euen and Donald have prepared me a place above, Isobel. I am more than ready for what will come.'

At the mention of his children and wife, lost in the Greek Fire during the second siege, a new fury surfaced. She wished she might have responded in the same vein, with Alisdair already gone before her and her heart promised into his care, but the silver coin burnt into the flesh at her breast with its own missive of loss.

She had not lain with a man and felt the earth move her. She had not quickened with child or known her breasts swell with milk. She had not travelled west past Dunfermline or taken a boat to a distant far shore.

It was not enough to die yet!

The scar that crossed her cheek smarted with the waste, ticking heavily to its own rhythm. She knew that Andrew would have seen the movement, but had become adept at the art of not noticing. If she had been the sort of woman who enjoyed the touch of others, she might have lain her fingers on his arm in thanks, but she was not that sort of woman. When the agitation settled she began to speak again.

'We are as prepared as we ever will be. Ian has the men on the targets each day and they seldom miss their mark.'

'The supplies are in, too. A good three months of salted meat and vegetables in the cellars.'

Three months. They would never last so long under such an onslaught. Observing Andrew, she saw truth beneath the banter. It was in his eyes and his stance and in the bloodied bandage he had not explained.

'What happened?'

'It is always prudent to stem the talk of defeat at its roots.'

'And did you?'

'I am getting older, Isobel, and the years of life I have enjoyed are beginning to count against me. There are men here who are young and hungry for the living they might not be able to do if—'

He stopped, the words lost in the wind between them, swirling away on the eddies of coldness into silence.

If?

When!

Had she not been standing here doing just as those soldiers did? Dreaming of more.

The coin lay against her skin, but in the company of Andrew she did not dare to find it. The topic of Marc lay dormant like an unsaid curse.

'And the party sent to the Lindsays—are they returned yet?'

He shook his head. 'There is little hope for any last-minute alliance, even given your sweetener, Isobel.'

She smiled at that. 'If the gold could have helped…'

'There is still time for some to leave with its succour. The boats are seaworthy.'

'Of course. The women must go and the children. Whatever room is left after that…perhaps the old might follow.'

'And you, Isobel. What of you?'

'Ceann Gronna is my home as no other place could be.'

'Yet if they capture you and do not kill you? You are hated in Edinburgh and the punishments of those pitting themselves against David have been severe.'

'They will not take me alive. Have no worry on that score.'

He swore loudly, something he seldom did.

'I pledge on the soul of Our Lord that we will not make it easy for them to take the keep. Every one of us shall harry ten of theirs into the afterlife.'

Nodding, she met his glance full on. 'I want to be on the battlements, too. I want to fight alongside you.'

She had not done that before. In the other sieges she had been the one running the keep's defences from the background. But Andrew had taught her the ways of battle as well as any man and for this campaign she needed to be there, sword in hand, death in hand.

She was relieved when he acquiesced, the struggle of trying to hide her intentions no longer necessary. Already she had had the armourer fashion a helmet and chain mail; she had a powerful bow, almost as tall as she was and made of yew, the arrows fitted with dyed goose-feather fletching in the shades of yellow and red.

If the tunnels to the sea were not breached, then they had a chance, for the concentric walls of Ceann

Gronna were thick and strong, those on the upper levels built for the defence of the lower ones.

Isobel's heartbeat quickened. Did she really dare to hope that they might yet survive this?

Two hundred men! Sometimes she dreamed of an emissary of the king riding in with terms of clemency. If they could hold out just this one more time, could it happen?

On the horizon she saw dust as the party sent to the Lindsay chief came into view, the standard of Ceann Gronna held high.

'Will you meet them with me?' she said to Andrew as she turned for the steps that led down into the hall.

Sir Marc de Courtenay sat in the dining chamber of the great royal castle on the Edinburgh hill of basalt and surveyed the scene before him.

A great many lords and their ladies dressed in all manner of finery dined on banqueting tables covered in crisp white linen.

The king sat beside him, his laugh booming across the room as the Lord of Glencoe related a tale of two young squires and their dogs. Marc himself had ceased to listen a good brace of minutes back.

The Last Supper. The final night before they set out tomorrow for Fife and the recalcitrant Ceann Gronna keep.

The messes before him offered soup and cygnets, eels and lampreys, roast goose, pheasants, swan and pies. The plate he ate from was of pure gold and his cup was overfilled with wine.

But he could not settle. He could not laugh at the descriptions of what the triumphant Loyalists might do to the Dalceann bitch.

The danger made his blood congeal as he chewed the goose meat without savouring it. The prospect of war had long ceased to leave any taste save bitterness in his mouth.

'Odds are we will be back here enjoying another banquet before summer is at its fullest.' Archibald McQuarry's tone was certain and gave no hint of the failure that had taken his oldest brother's life. He was a sour man of poor humour, a man Marc had not warmed to in the slightest.

'You have experience, then, of such campaigns,' Marc countered, knowing full well that he had not.

The other shook his head as he upended his glass. 'Your knowledge of warfare is unrivalled in all Christianity and you are the favourite of the king.' The words were said with an undercurrent of spite and foolishness, a lord who hated anyone rising through the ranks of life by sheer hard work and persistence.

It was the wine speaking, Marc surmised, and the inbuilt pretension that seemed to separate nobility from the masses. The blood of a lord flowed through his own veins, too, but a dozen hard-fought battles had cured him for ever of such vanity. Part of him was pleased that he had been saddled with two men who would be easily manoeuvred. It would make the job of what he had to do so much easier. He caught the eye of David, who in turn grabbed his arm, laying his hand hard upon his sleeve before raising the goblet he drank from.

'To Sir Marc de Courtenay, sent to help Scotland under the Auld Alliance and one of the finest knights who ever rode into battle beneath my banner.'

The sound of cheering lifted to the rafters. How easy it was to mould and shape the opinions of men.

'And to King Philip the Sixth of France who allowed you leave from the army of Burgundy to bring us support.'

Again the crowd bayed until David gestured silence.

'The man who steals back the Devil's tooth around Isobel Dalceann's neck shall be rewarded well. Mark my words, my lords. I want her blood spilled sure and sweet on to the earth of Ceann Gronna, a warning against all others who might secretly harbour an ill thought of intent.'

The entourage stood at such rhetoric, feet marking the beat of victory and hands using the heavy butt of eating knives to underline pleasure.

Outside through the window of glass the sun draped the room in light. It glinted on Anne of Kinburn's flaxen hair as she raised her tumbler to him.

Marc pushed down relief. The words of the king

still left him leeway. He had not mentioned the death of a traitor. Another hour and the waiting would be over. One more night and he would be gone.

Chapter Seven

It had begun!

The men moving towards Ceann Gronna across the greenness of the low hills in the distance kept coming, swarming like bees from the east. Isobel could see the great banners of the king held aloft on the far plateau, the gold lion of Scotland on a background of burgundy, blowing gentle against the breezes of springtime.

Two hundred men. She had never seen so many in one place and at one time melded together by mail and the colours of war.

The machinery of a siege came, too, the trebuchets with weights and slings and the mangonels, thick bands of twisted cords on the spools of the hurling arms. Oxen pulled them, yoked to the wooden carts in groups of four so heavy was the burden. Tomorrow they would be positioned closer once the commander had seen the lay of the land, the weak spots noted and the tactics drawn.

Her eyes skirted across the countryside as she put herself in the position of her enemy.

The square walls could be used to hold the belfries and the postern to one side of the keep was thinly protected.

On the brow of the hill striped tents were being erected, the flags of royalty marking them as David's, the trees at the foot of the incline protecting them from wind and rain off the sea.

Already the fires had begun. The cottages near the river were well alight, plumes of thick red flame and black smoke pulling upwards.

'They will surround us by the afternoon,' Angus noted, 'although the sea aspect will stay safe at least.'

'Thank God for the cliffs.' Andrew made the sign of the cross as he said it.

Isobel knew there would be no talk of ransom. Ceann Gronna would be sacked and those within the walls killed. She was glad most of the women and all of the children had left by boat, waiting it out in the lands across the border in England with most of the French gold as their surety.

Over the valley she saw a small group of men on horses watching them.

The commanders. She had heard that there were three of them and word had filtered into Fife that their supreme leader was the most experienced fighter in all of Christendom. Her eyes scanned carefully, but there was no distinguishing feature discernible from this distance. Perhaps it was for the best. She did not wish to toss and turn tonight in her cot with the visage of those who would kill her keeping her from sleep. She would see them soon enough. Such a thought made it hard to breathe.

'I have men in the woods behind them. They will come through the tunnel from the beach this evening after dark and report all that they have seen.' Ian shoved his sword through a slitted window on the wooden hoardings, tilting it so that the sunlight glinted on the blade. A declaration of intent.

Seeing an answering flash of light, Andrew scuffed at the wood beneath their feet. 'Come closer, lad, and see what I have to give you,' he jibed.

A trail of soldiers on horses wound their way down the path to the river, lances held close as they disappeared behind the thin cover of bush to be lost in a cloud of smoke coming in from the sea.

'They have found the tithe barn,' she said softly, knowing that it was ablaze from the direction of the wind. Cinders swirled in the heat, creating a new worry of fire.

'Dusk is an hour away,' Andrew said. 'They will dig in till the morrow after the sun is down.'

'Or use it to their advantage,' Ian retorted.

Isobel thought of the bowls of water placed just inside the outer walls. If they rippled, it meant tunnels were being dug. With a force this size she expected that to happen and had set the few women left in the keep to watch for any sign of movement.

No one would help them. The Lindsays had sent word that whilst they understood the plight of the Dalceann clan they could not be a party to such direct insult to the king. The Woods and Wemys had said the same.

The ancient patriarchal system of governance in Scotland was gone, the chief and the right of clan law lost to the new view of Crown ownership. Only in acquiescence was there defence. Lord, that her father could have worked this out by the defeat of other keeps, but Ceann Gronna had been the first to refuse the royal ordinance and as such was a shining example of what not to do. Ancient families had seen the strength of the king's soldiers and capitulated, just as Alisdair had bidden her father do all those years before.

If this siege did not take them, the next one would, though, looking at the size and strength of those that were streaming on to the Dalceann land, Isobel knew in her bones that it would only be a matter of time before they failed.

She failed.

The thought crossed her mind of simply walking out herself and surrendering, on the promise of safety for all that were left inside, but Andrew and she had had this talk before and it was his view that no pledge for leniency would be honoured.

She despised them, this marauding force, these minions of a king who gave no heed to an ancient possession. She loathed that they would kill men and women who had protected this part of Scotland for hundreds of years and more, clan people with the same language as those who would smite them, the same religious beliefs and the same love of country.

A horn sounded from across the valley, baneful in its tone, regrouping men perhaps or just a reminder of menace. She suspected the latter as the sound echoed against the Ceann Gronna stone.

The keep from this angle looked far more fragile than Marc remembered it.

As his horse moved to the blast of a horn from close by he wondered how the castle could have ever weathered two sustained attacks. Huntworth and Glencoe had been full of the methods they might use in their offensive and Marc could see that the line of fire they had come up with might just work.

Concentrating on the castle, he watched the people on the wooden hourds above the inner wall. The flash of a sword had caught his eye a few moments ago, deliberate probably in its message of provocation. He knew from the intelligence on the way here that many of the Dalceann clan had been sent away on the longboats for England. He hoped like hell that Isobel Dalceann was amongst them, safe and sound from the ire of a king. His gut instinct told him that she would not be, however, and that she was there now, looking out at him and plotting ways to make every life the keep would lose worth its weight in the blood of her enemy.

Him. The enemy. Aye, she would hate him soon enough.

The arrow came from the land to the left, he was to think later, where a thick stand of trees hid the castle from a group of tents placed in the lee of the wind.

It came at a height that might have killed him easily had he not bent at that particular moment to tighten his right footstrap. It twanged into the wide edge of his shield and pierced through two layers of leather and one of wood. As he was not wearing a helmet, he could only imagine what it would have done to his head had the aim been true.

Breaking off the fletching, he looked down at its markings. A king's arrow! Mariner, his second-in-command, had seen the danger and now galloped up to him from further afield, his face full of question.

'It did not come from the keep,' he said, even as Marc handed him the arrow.

'Then we have someone in our midst who would wish me dead,' Marc answered,

'Hell, it's hard enough to mount a siege without having to look over your shoulders.' Callum Mariner looked worried.

'So let us hope this has put him off from trying again.'

* * *

Later that day as Marc returned to his tent he saw Huntworth watching him from a hill above in a manner that was unsettling. There was something about Archibald McQuarry that worried him. A man who held a grudge about being the second-in-command, perhaps? A lord who could not see it in himself to take orders from another sent by a foreign king to Scotland in order to make certain the Auld Alliance was being adhered to.

The incident of the arrow came to mind unbidden. Could he have tried to kill him?

He made a mental note to watch Huntworth carefully and to make certain that his own back remained protected.

Marc was tired of seeing the mangonels hurling their missiles against an ever-increasingly fragile Ceann Gronna, of hearing the groan of timber and the heavy fall of stone.

Lord God, please let Isobel be away from the wooden hourdings and safe inside the inner wall, for if she was anywhere near the battlements… He made himself stop even as his eyes kept searching for a figure with a long silken swathe of black hair. With the full helmets and heavy mail he could not distinguish one from the other, but the worry in him wound into his blood like a curse.

Why did the keep not just surrender, raise the flag

of truce and take their chances within the system of Scottish law? At this rate of attrition they would all be dead in a matter of weeks and nothing much that he could do about it.

His soldiers had taken a pounding, too, but the fires in the timber defences on the roof of Ceann Gronna spewed flame and smoke into the bowels of the castle.

Where the hell was she? Could she have left by the sea tunnels she had spoken of? He swore beneath his breath because he knew she would not leave until the end, her beloved keep and clan as precious as life itself.

He hoped Andrew or Ian might have the sense to make her stay somewhere away from danger, but even that thought was swallowed up by another.

Isobel Dalceann would fight, he knew it, sword and shield in hand until she fell. The image of her trampled and broken made him swallow back fear, the ache in his throat threatening breath.

Two weeks had passed since the first assault on the keep and already the outer wall was in danger of being breached by the belfry. At the foot of stone many fallen soldiers lay, face down where death had taken them, left in the elements while others took up their place. Angus lay amongst them.

'Another day or two and we will have lost,' Andrew muttered at her side and Ian scowled back at the words.

'Keep talking like that, old man, and we might as well lay our arms down now,' he said, his bow letting loose an arrow from the quiver he had at his side.

Isobel's glance went to the hills further beyond the encampment. If only help would come, she thought, if only she might spy some glinting armour of an allied force in the distance.

But there was nothing.

Her world turned on the moments left to them, less and less given the position of the belfry, its body swathed in wet cattle skins so that the Dalceann fire might not harm it.

The noise of battle had dimmed, too, a quieter ferocity than the out-and-out chaos of the days past.

Not long.

Her fingers crept to the coin at her throat.

Marc took fifteen of his best men and gestured them to follow through the sea path and around the edge of the sheer cliff that rose up into the limed white walls of Ceann Gronna.

He knew the way, for he had scouted out this entrance on the second day of arriving here, the door that blocked the path proving little obstacle to a man who had picked the locks of some of the most important portals in Europe. There were no boats. He had seen that, too, gone probably with those who had left for the safety of England before spring.

The ladders further up surprised him, built from stone and from sea-smoothed wood, circling up into the cliff, the rope they sported as handles strong and knotted. For purchase.

Waving his men on, he took the lead, his anger at the situation he now found himself in fuelling his pace. Huntworth and Glencoe were bumbling fools and king's men, yet they had almost managed to breach the keep at Ceann Gronna. He could afford to tarry no longer for if they got to Isobel Dalceann first…?

No, he would not think like that.

The water below them surged into the rock face, the remnants of spray hurling upwards, soaking their mail and tabards.

Another hundred yards. He could hear the shouts of battle from here, the triumphant cries of force quelling what little was left of the resistance of strong walls. His feet raced across the remaining distance and he used the strength of his body to break down the flimsy gate guarding Ceann Gronna to the south.

And then they were in, running along the stone cellars and the bottle pantries before rising up to the service passages and the kitchen beside the Great Hall.

They dealt with resistance as they went, easily and

quickly, the astonished faces of the Dalceann men holding no weight against them.

Already he had caught a glimpse of those wearing the colours of Glencoe on the battlements above through the stained-glass windows. His heartbeat faltered in an unexpected panic.

God. Where the hell was she? A group of serving maids pressed together beneath the high table, their faces blotched red in fear, and he signalled to his men to leave them be.

Beyond the hall he heard raised voices and the running of feet. The private chambers of Ceann Gronna were dressed in large tapestries, the unicorns and magical beasts portrayed behind chests of oak and brass. Windows let in the light through narrow lattices. Isobel's own room he recognised from the last time he had been here, more frugal than the others, two painted linen hangings keeping draughts at bay.

Nowhere. She was nowhere to be seen, though a woman's shout had him turning and there she was, between Andrew and Ian, back to the wall as she beat off a group of mailed enemy streaming in from the belfry.

No lightweight defence, either, her blade dancing in the slanted sunlight coming from a wide door, catching her hair, which swirled in effort, a raven-black curtain of silk shot through with the darkest of red. A pain of want sliced through hesitation, an easy pathway against all the reasons of why he should just turn and leave her here to the destiny of her rebellion. The breath he took congealed into stillness, every sinew in his body understanding that he needed to take care, for even the slightest of mistakes would consign her to the afterworld, the beleaguered standards of Dalceann spilling through careless hands into death. He saw her sword dip and the muscles of her arm slacken, her neck bare and exposed.

'Nooooo.' Shaking his head, he let her gaze touch his, eyes reddened from fear or exhaustion, he knew not which, a mark of charcoal curled on to her forehead in a stripe.

He knew the instant she registered that it was him beneath the helmet, for her pupils widened, bitter anger and unslaked rage threaded with another emotion.

Disbelief.

Her fighting hand was awash with thickened blood, her mail torn above the elbow and the skin exposed, the remnants of a thin white kirtle soaked in red.

She wore no gauntlets or helmet, no protection to ward off danger. The arrogance of such actions winded him with fury.

The stone behind was cold and smooth—her last tactile memory, perhaps, before she left this world for the next one.

Her arm ached, too, the wash of red making it

harder to hold her sword; she knew she should never have removed the gauntlets.

They had broken through and flooded into the castle just as she had sat down for a rest. She had not had the time to gather her gloves or headgear, but had been caught in the flight downstairs to the solar where she now fought back against the wall and as many of the enemy that could fit into the small round room before her.

A mistake. Better to have fled for the passages to the sea and taken her chance that way, water allowing one a death that she had heard was gentle.

She had meant to do it such.

But here they would not take her alive, either, the heavy points of steel slicing through the air with a deft quickness. If she should relax her guard and tip her throat up to the blade…

'Nooo.'

A keening cry of fury rent the air around her, turning the hairs on her arms up into panic as her eyes caught sight of the only one she had thought never to see again.

Marc!

Here.

In the mail of King David, sword tipped red.

A traitor and a betrayer; a man who would leave the keep of Ceann Gronna with secrets in his head to return a brace of months later and use them against those who had only been kind.

A payment of death for the gift of life. She could smell the sea spray on him as he jostled closer, his eyes cold with the knowledge of retribution and deceit. Drawing her sword up, she tried to use it on him, but Andrew got there first, his blade swinging through the air to be met by a parry and a feint.

He didn't stand a chance. It was like watching a child against a war-toughened knight, the sun catching silver as Marc used the blunt end of his scabbard and rammed it down across Andrew's head. He might have lived, she thought, had not the soldier behind finished the job, his blade ending that which Marc had begun.

She screamed his name even as his blood seeped on to the flagstones of the inner solar, small streams of it tracing along the dents of mortar to pool into red against the wall.

The heart of her sorrow clawed into grief and horror and then acceptance as Marc again lifted his blade.

This time it was for her.

She did not even try to fight him or place any resistance against such an ending. It was over. The king had won.

Then everything slowed: the heavy pull as she was knocked back behind Marc the Betrayer, the head of a soldier she did not know rolling like a ball over and over and over.

Nothing made sense.

Ian was dead, for she had seen him fall, but others sent by David lay there, too, entwined together under the blade of the man whose silver coin she carried around her neck.

His own private army, she thought, as she tried to reconcile why she was still alive and all the rest were dead, save the soldiers she had seen him arrive with. A double crossing, perhaps, with the thought of profit at stake and a hidden cache of gold for the taking?

There was silence save for the heavy breathing of men in chain mail who stood to listen to the battering ram on the front gate, sweat running down their faces.

Then more of David's soldiers, as the oaken doors to the Great Hall were forced apart and a sea of burgundy and gold streamed into Ceann Gronna unhindered.

'She is mine. I claim her.' Marc had his knife in hand as he raised it in intent, just as he had done once in the forest above Kirkcaldy.

No protection in this, though. All she could feel was the hatred.

When she turned to fight him he ripped the bib of her mail upwards, fingers clamped about the coin at her throat as though he had known it to be there, the chain hanging from either side of his palm as he raised it in the air, silver hidden in his grasp.

'The Dalceann witch is mine. I claim her in the name of David and in the name of the Underlord.'

A cheer went up, loud and resounding, and a tunnel of darkness came towards her as Marc the Betrayer pressed down against the exposed side of her neck with his war-hardened fingers.

She was unconscious, for at least the time it would take to get her from the solar to the room he had used last time he was here. Once there, he laid her on the bed, then opened the hidden safe, giving his followers the gold to take to the room he would use. 'Guard it well,' he said. 'Some of you remain in the corridor to guard this room, too.' They nodded in acquiescence.

He closed the door behind them, allowing the fall of heavy slats across pinioned hardwood to secure the entrance.

His breathing was rough and he was sweating, the drops running into his eyes with their stinging saltiness.

Thank God. A little sanctuary. A small window of time before the questions came. He would need to be ready and Isobel Dalceann would need to hate him if this was to work. No soft redress or whispered explanation. Her life hung in the balance; even the slightest perception of complicity would kill her and his men. His actions here and in the solar had to look like a hostage taken in the heat of battle under the direct orders of a king.

Shaking her awake, he slapped the cheek without the scar and let her go when she exploded into fury.

She was strong, he would give her that as she went for him, talons out and teeth bared.

'You…you…bastard.'

Her breath barely allowed her the saying of it and she lunged again as he moved away, holding out his hand in a small warning.

'Stay back.'

'Why?' Her voice broke as she continued. 'Because you want to kill me, too? Or because you would bed me?' She screamed the last words, her breasts beneath the heavy mail heaving in wrath.

'I draw the line at raping women,' he returned and liked the way she drew herself up at that. A fighting Isobel would be so much easier to protect than a frightened one.

'I highly doubt that you have the morals to draw a line on anything.' She snarled the reply.

'You might be surprised, Lady Dalceann, at just what I do hold true.'

The knife was out before he had a chance to see it, whistling past his ear with all the expertise of one well trained in its use. An inch to the left and he would have been dead. In pure instinct he knocked her throwing arm hard and she fell roughly against the stool by the window, catching her head against the stone overhang.

'I hate you.' Not even anger was left in the flatness of her voice.

This time she stayed down.

'Good.' He turned to the door, collecting her knife as he went, the fury in him demanding a release from the room that held so much in deceit and so little in truth.

Outside he turned the heavy key and pocketed it, leaving eight of his men on guard in the corridor.

'Let nobody in or out,' he instructed. 'I shall be back in less than an hour.'

Striding away, he found a small overhang on the battlements hidden from any view and leant back against the solid and limed Ceann Gronna stone. The wind off the Firth was in his face, fresh and exhilarating, and he tipped up his chin to feel it better.

The coin she had worn around her throat was wrapped into the flesh of his palm, as warm as it had been when he had taken it from her, and he opened his fingers to look.

She had made an ornament of it and threaded it on to plaited silver. His coin. His memory? A thousand thoughts piled in upon the first one. Why the hell would she be wearing such a reminder of him?

Lifting his other hand, he slammed it hard against the stone until tears ran into his eyes. Andrew was dead and Ian and a number of other faces he remembered from the clearing in the forest. He could not have saved them all and saved her as well, but she would never understand such a thing.

The acrid smell of smoke covered everything.

Chapter Eight

The shaking surprised her, for she seldom allowed emotion to rule her the way it was doing now. It ran in tremors from her teeth to her fingers and down into her stomach and legs. No control over any of it.

Clutching at the stool, she raised herself with her good arm, walking to her bed and sitting down. Her head ached and where she had bitten through her bottom lip the swelling throbbed as she tasted blood.

What was happening outside? Had they killed everyone? Would they bury Andrew?

Anguish made her swallow, the bile of memory bitter in her mouth.

Betrayed and forsaken, the future hewn out before her in uncertainty. She had heard that they hanged people like her, traitors to a king, stretched across the public places and disembowelled alive.

Her fingers went of their own accord to the silver coin at her throat before she stopped them. The trinket was as lost as her dreams, stupid dreams of love, family and accord. Once she had imagined Marc would come back riding through the mist to save her, and now…?

He was the king's commander brought to Ceann Gronna because of his knowledge of the place. Fourteen days and the keep was gone. He would pay for such a treachery, she swore that he would.

How?

The wheels of her mind turned quickly, but as another thought struck her she moved to open the stone that concealed her safe.

The gold had been taken!

It was Marc's doing, she was sure of it, the lure of treasure a heady reward for sacking the Dalceann keep.

Traitorous *and* greedy! The disappointment that flowered under anger was enough to make her throw the stool against the wall, shattering a ewer in the process. The fragments of tiny shards littered the floor and she liked the sound of crushed pottery beneath her boots as she walked across them.

He returned just as dusk was falling, the tasks of war after victory taking longer than he had thought they would.

He had replaced the coin that he had taken from her neck with a tooth he had found in the back room of a little-known goldsmith, after scouring Edinburgh. It was exactly the sort that would invoke the old magic of a sorceress, the clasp engraved in some ancient language and the sheen of it yellowed. Just another protection, a further proof. He would unveil it when he needed to. In the courts of Philip he had been long tutored in the art of showmanship and its uses, and superstitions were easily manoeuvred.

She was asleep when he entered, her chain mail bundled at the bottom of her bed, and there were pieces of blue pottery vase all over the floor. He nudged as many as he could beneath the bed as he walked and shook her awake.

Her dark eyes opened instantly, hooded in hatred. He lit no reed and the fireplace in the chamber was empty, leaving the room so cold he could see his breath.

Hell. The heart of all this was eating at him with its wrongness, but he made himself reach into his jacket and pull out the rope.

She shot upwards at the sight of it but it was far too late. He had the bindings around her wrist before she could even struggle and with little effort turned her over to fasten them behind her back.

She lay still then, panting. He felt his hands on the outline of her bottom.

'You are my captive, Lady Dalceann, and the king's enemy. One wrong move and…'

I cannot save you. He had almost said it. The idea of such a mistake made him stiffen.

'And I will die.' She finished the words herself,

her tongue licking away the dryness from her lips. The long line of her neck was pale in the oncoming evening, the pulse of blood beating fast against skin. Placing one finger against the warmth, he listened. Too hot and too rapid. His glance took in the wound on her arm. Untended for how many hours?

Not quite as easy as he had hoped, then, as he tore back the sleeve and applied a salve he always kept on him.

Rising, he removed his surcoat and pulled off his tunic, leaving only the hose. He saw in her eyes exactly what she thought he might do to her next. So easy to play the villain when a woman looked as this one did. The scar on her damaged cheek was raised and her lashes were so long and thick the shadows of them almost met it.

'I can tie you to the bed, too, if that is what is required,' he warned.

Imagining her shackled thus, but in much more pleasant and sensual surroundings, his cock rose and he knew she had seen the movement when she began to kick.

'No.' The word was so fearful he swore beneath his breath. If his men were to burst through the door and find her like this, he doubted that he would be able to moderate their reactions, for Isobel Dalceann was so very beautiful.

He was pleased when she stilled, for her shirt had fallen across the line of her breast as she struggled

and without the use of her hands she could not re-
fasten it. Each movement brought her nipple more
clearly into view.

'Keep still.'

The power of her body angered him and he threw
a blanket that lay on the chest across her, covering
temptation.

She was a witch even bound and hurt. Every story
he had ever heard of her had been true.

He would rape her tonight, in the dark. The very
thought of it made Isobel sick. Already he had removed his clothes, the tight engorgement in his hose
letting her understand the way his thoughts had wandered.

She tugged at her bindings under the cover, a useless pursuit as the struggle tightened the ropes instead
of loosening them. She imagined him removing her
lad's pants and entering her from behind, his visage unseen, breaking the last of any trust left between them.

Why had she ever dreamt of him, hoping that he
might come with an army to save her? This betrayal
made everything worse.

Moderating her breathing so that he would not
realise how scared she was, she watched as he laid
a tapestry ripped from the wall on the floor next to
the door. The yellow threads of the unicorn's eyes
met hers and she remembered stitching the piece

when she had been younger, before the war arrived at Ceann Gronna.

What did he mean to do with it now? She saw he placed his knife and sword beside the fabric. Both weapons had been cleaned and burnished with oil for protection, each blade razor sharp. Beside them lay another bolt of rope, neatly turned and looped, stronger even than the cords around her wrists.

Folding his tunic into a square, he simply lay down, arms behind his head as a pillow and eyes closed against the room. His body in the dim light was muscle honed and bronzed, the sizeable scar she had noticed before at Ceann Gronna when he was ill running up the left side of his ribs.

Was this a trick? She turned to watch him better and the rustle of the blanket brought his eyes back to her own. She saw the glint of green through shadow.

'Do not move from the bed, Isobel.'

His voice told her that the warning he gave was no idle threat, the hard planes of his cheek dirtied by the toil of battle. He looked tired, older, the lines around his eyes deeper than she remembered them.

He would not sleep on top of her, then, and exact the payment that all vanquishing victors expected of women?

He would not toss her out on to a pallet on the floor, uncomfortably cold with the late spring winds from the north still blowing hard?

The blanket she lay under was a cocoon of

warmth and her bed was soft, her pillow allowing her the repose of an easy sleep even given the constraints around her hands. Marc the Betrayer had nothing on him save the dirtied tunic which he had recently disposed of and now dragged over himself as a covering.

Silence coated the room, thick and forced, as outside the voices of soldiers lingering on the upper ramparts floated in an eerie echo.

Neither her men nor her allies! The very thought of the plunder and sacking of her home had her turning to the wall. Andrew was dead. She kept perfectly still as tears trailed down her cheeks to be absorbed by the cotton cover wrapped around the bolster, a wet reminder of all that she had lost and would never have again.

He knew she cried. He could see it in the shake of her shoulders and the small tremors through the blanket.

So many damned men dead! The last look of the one they named Andrew replayed in his head over and over. A good man. A gentle man. A man who had seen him safe across the countryside into the hands of the ferryman.

If he could have saved him he would have, but had he not countered the threat, then all hope for Isobel would have been lost.

He prayed that her minion might know of his sacrifice from wherever it was his spirit now lingered. In such logic he found absolution.

'You came by the sea tunnels, did you not?'

Her question surprised him a good half an hour later, for although sleep had not come to him he thought she had found repose.

'Indeed.'

'How is it, then, that you are called in the court of King David the Second?'

'Marc de Courtenay.'

'And James? Was that a lie, too?'

'Nay, it is my second name.'

'I should never have dragged you in from the sea, Marc James de Courtenay.' Flat certainty lay in her words. 'Andrew did beseech me to throw you off the eastern ramparts. He said you were dangerous and that Ceann Gronna would be best rid of you. If I had listened, he might still be alive.'

'If it was not I who captured you first, it would have been others, and, believe it or not, they most surely would have been less concerned for your welfare than I am.'

Marc thought of Glencoe and Huntworth and the conversation he had endured with them earlier in the evening. They thought the spoils of war should be shared equally and the beauty of Isobel Dalceann did her no favours. Nay, with dark hair to the waist and her gold-rimmed eyes, he imagined her passed around the triumphant commanders like a bone. It was only by laying down the law that she was in here with him, still safe, the authority in his actions silencing argument.

He did not know how long he could keep her safe, for the morrow would bring new questions and the number of his men was not as great as that of the combined forces of the others. He had left none of McQuarry's men alive in the solar, but the windows may have let in other eyes and what they might have seen could compromise everything.

'Is there water?' Her query broke through worry, a note in her voice that sounded defeated and frightened.

Rising, he collected the skin he kept filled.

'Sit up.'

She did so with difficulty, her sagging cotton kirtle exposing more of her womanly curves. When she saw where he looked she held his gaze. Her nipples were dark in the half-light, budding atop breasts that were firm and generous. She drank only lightly from the pouch; when she was finished she tipped up her chin.

'Untie me, Marc. Please.' The lids of her eyes were hooded, her lips apart as she rounded her shoulders further. 'Perhaps then we could find a way to enjoy tonight if tomorrow might never arrive for me? There was a time that I thought you liked me, after all…'

The look in her eyes almost fooled him as she arched back, the heat of sex in the space between them.

The promise on her face was beguiling. *Take me if you dare to,* it said, though another truth also lingered. He could almost feel her fingers on the hilt of his knife plunging it into his chest.

Breaking contact, he stood and moved away from the bed, opening the latticed window so that the cold streamed in upon him.

'God, you nearly had me believing you.' He dug his nails into the bare skin of his arms, taking the prick of pain with a satisfaction. 'And what a mistake that would have been.'

Her expression had changed entirely. Now pure hatred laced her eyes. 'Traitor.' Her voice drifted across to him without any hint of uncertainty. 'I will kill you when I get the chance. I swear I will, Marc the Betrayer.'

He laughed, though he had not meant to, and, looking around, saw the blanket was tightly pulled up around her neck.

The roar of the sea came up from below, tumbling waves of an endless ocean, and the clouds blowing in from the Kingdom of Norway were thick and cold. Tomorrow it would rain, a fact that brought with it another set of problems.

Ensconced inside the castle, an invading army would be restless and the patience of men stretched.

Lady Isobel Dalceann would have to be kept in her chamber until the weather cleared and he would be trapped for great lengths of time in here with her. Even the thought made him tired.

'Go to sleep,' he said, lying down again on his pallet, 'for you will need all the rest you can get to face tomorrow.'

She thought of her father and of Alisdair and the days of summer long past when she had not known how to kill a man or play the whore.

Anger at her whole stupid ploy of seduction gave her no peace for sleep. She was useless at the pretence anyway, with the vivid scar on her face and her boy's clothes. Her arm ached, a dull never-ending throb, worsened by her inability to stretch it out. Her lips were dry.

Marc breathed deeply. She had listened to his breathing even out a good hour ago and he had not moved his position for all of that time. Asleep. The weaponry at his side beckoned to her, the outline of sharpened steel still visible even in the nighttime darkness.

She moved to the edge of the bed and then stopped. Nothing.

Rolling back the blanket, she slowly sat up, her feet now across the side of the mattress, almost at the floor.

'One more step and I use the rope.'

The quiet of his words made her jump, more menacing in the calm than they could ever have been in a shout, the cold seeping into her bones with a stealth that annoyed her.

She would abandon her fight for the feel of wool around her shoulders. Her arms hugged her body as she tried to catch on to any remaining heat. The shivers in her legs reached up to her stomach and then into her words.

'What will h-happen to me? Tomorrow?'

'Hopefully what has been forthcoming today! The sanctuary of this room and the ability to remain isolated should afford you some respite.'

'From…?'

'Your keep has found itself at cross-purposes with the king. I find, in general, that traitors are not given much in the way of a second chance.'

'Even though I gave you one…'

Anger now replaced an indifferent tone. 'If you relate anything of such a personal nature to those outside this room, Lady Dalceann, I could not stop them from killing you.'

'You would want to?'

'Cold-blooded murder has no place in a system of justice.'

'What of betrayal?'

'Is it my actions you speak of or the edicts of the new feudal land laws? In my mind both are linked.'

Too clever, she thought. Answer yes to either and she was damned.

'You have been in Scotland for only a little while and yet you presume to know the ancient history of Fife?'

She stood as she said it, feet firmly planted on the floor. 'You come back to Ceann Gronna with your false ideas of valour and faith, a man who would bite the hand of those who helped him? Nay, worse,' she added, logic and sense dismissed by plain grief and fury, 'plunge your scabbard down on to the head of a good and kind man under the guise of the backing of the law to enforce such resistance?'

She saw him rise, forming a barrier in front of his sword and knife, his chest naked and his hose pulled low where the lacings had loosened.

Not a man fashioned by lethargy or excess. His beauty was unequivocal and indisputable. Isobel hated the knowledge and the way it lessened her anger and bridled her hate. All she wanted was the fury back.

They were alike, she and Marc, she suddenly thought, alike in their allegiances to ideas no longer tenable. No one could win here; in the struggle for the keep, Ceann Gronna would be lost stone by stone into the hands of a king who had never deserved it.

Hopelessness rushed in on the heels of impotence. Fourteen days of fighting, to come to this impasse, personal and vapid. Andrew and the others should not have died for such a useless rebellion.

Staying still, she breathed out, hard. 'What would it take to strike a bargain with you?'

'A bargain for your life?'

She laughed because his question was so very banal. 'My life is over already. It is the lives of those left at Ceann Gronna that I would plead for.'

'With what?'

'Gold. More than you could ever imagine.'

'Here?'

'Much more than that in the safe.'

'There are other cachets?'

She remained mute, watching as the wheels of his mind turned in his eyes. Finally he spoke.

'Perhaps it might be enough for a king mired in debt.'

'To save everyone left at Ceann Gronna?'

He nodded.

Lord, Marc thought. It could work. Gold had its own language, after all, and if what she promised was true...?

'Where are they? Those of my people still alive from the battle?'

The woman who had plucked him from the sea materialised out of the girl bound in this room, like magic, as she turned her damaged cheek towards him.

'They are in the dungeons guarded by my men.'

'Who are the others, then, who have come with you?'

'Huntworth and Glencoe.' Her face paled considerably and Marc knew she had made the connections, but he was tired of lying to her.

'Huntworth? One of the commanders that came before?'

'Nay, his brother, Archibald McQuarry. You killed the first lord of the title.'

'Then he has no cause to like me.'

She sat down on the bed. Dried blood the colour of rust stained her torn kirtle.

Nearly dawn. The first callings of birdsong rent the air, above the sound of the waves from the sea. Her hair dropped around her shoulders to the line of her hips, touching the bedsheets in places with its wild and uneven length. Like the silk of night. With her full lips and her tip-tilt nose she reminded him of a painting he had once seen in the royal palace of Philip. Not an angel, but a wanton siren, beckoning men to do things that they had no will for.

He wished he might just undress her and take her, here in this room, politics melded under a kinder promise and all the time in the world to make her understand the danger and the hope and the way a man might protect a woman.

For ever.

He imagined his fingers stroking her belly and falling lower, into the hidden promise of woman-hood. He imagined her warmth and her wetness and the way she might call out as he penetrated into the shocking need of lust.

'Isobel.' He said her name and she looked up, her glance brimming with an unsaid knowledge.

And silence stretched between them, caught in each other's eyes, the aftermath of violence, the comprehension of death, the joy of still living and the pull of something stronger, more primitive.

The buds of her nipples hardened under his gaze, twin peaks of darkness below linen. The line of her shoulders was stretched firmly back, the bindings tight. Easy to take. He knew she felt what he did when her breathing quickened.

His captive. His right. An hour or so till the day broke properly and a door that was well secured.

One coupling should do it, take the power that she wielded with her feminine wiles and render them impotent, for he seldom returned to a woman a second time.

Her tears stopped him, falling across her cheeks to run unhindered down to the blood-and dirt-stained kirtle. She did nothing to hide them and behind the dark of her gaze he saw a pain that was all of his making.

Swearing soundly, he moved his bedding from the doorway, collected his weapons and left the room.

Chapter Nine

Marc had felt like a youth in the first bud of libido, no sense in any of it and so very much to lose. He drained the ale from the pewter mug before him and then the one after that.

Had Isobel Dalceann done it deliberately? Had she used the spells she was rumoured to be so very good at to make him believe that she was a siren unequalled in her ability to give him the ease he craved? An unfulfilled and empty promise that laughed at him from a distance. His cock throbbed as he moved on the hard wooden bench.

'Did you tame the arrogant Dalceann witch, de Courtenay?' Huntworth sat beside him at the table, a heavy night's drinking showing in his face. 'Does she know now that her life is worth less than nothing here?'

'Aye, that she does.' Marc had to be careful in his answers, for Archibald McQuarry was known for his use of force and violence.

'Then bring her up to the Great Hall and give us the chance of a game or two. If she dies in the playing, I doubt David would care.'

'Aye, we could kill her—it would be an easy task and God knows she deserves it. But I have heard talk of riches at Ceann Gronna that we have not as yet found. Perhaps it might be more useful to keep her alive until we do?'

'What sort of riches?'

'Gold.' He brought forth a handful of the jewels taken from her room and laid them on the table, the promise of such largesse a potent persuader of men.

Both Huntworth and Glencoe stood to touch, turning the gold over and over as they felt the weight of the bounty. Marc knew he had them when the lust in their eyes was replaced by the more malleable emotion of greed.

'She kens where it is from, then?' McQuarry's voice held that particular note of avarice.

'I am certain that she must.' Marc made much of chewing around the bone of a tasty bit of beef and soaking the juices up with a trencher of bread before he continued. 'If you would give me a few more days with her…'

'Done.' Glencoe spoke for them both. 'Some bounty for David and some for us though, aye?'

The procession of shapely wenches coming from the kitchen with more food helped his stance, too. One or two of them caught Marc's glance, offering him more than just the bread and meat. Shaking away their interest, he watched as McQuarry's hand disappeared under the skirt of the prettiest girl, pulling her on to his lap and kissing her soundly.

He smiled because such encouragement was to be fostered and men riding the loins of willing companions would be less likely to remember the feisty and less amenable Lady Isobel Dalceann.

Even here, a hundred yards from her room, she still pulled at him, her full and sensual lips inviting an ease that promised enthralment.

Breathing out, he understood that the line he walked along narrowed even in the daylight. The gold would buy him some time, but he needed to have Lady Dalceann safely back to Edinburgh if he was to truly protect her.

Huntworth was his biggest problem. If he was to view Isobel properly in the light of day, Marc knew that trouble would ensue, for even in her lad's clothes and dirtied her beauty was barely tarnished.

He looked around to see where his men were in relation to those of the others. One group sat at the back of the hall, and another to one side. The soldiers of McQuarry were gathered around the long table that stretched from the front and they were unruly. Another worry!

The rain outside slanted into the keep from the sea, no light drizzle but a driving force that could be heard against the high windows on the eastern walls of the hall. It was cold for this time of the year, too, the spring muffled by a late wintry blast. He hoped that the blanket he had left Isobel with would be warm enough and that she would stay quietly in the chamber.

He would leave another group of his men to guard her, and he would strike out into the countryside in an hour or so to find a safe place to go to if there should be a need of it.

Isobel waited to see if Marc would return; when he did not she sat down on the bed, her arms aching with the effort needed to keep the bindings from pulling at her skin further.

She was amazed that she was not dead yet, or that Marc de Courtenay had not tired of the sexual tension between them and seen to the end of it.

Such desire was not new to her, these looks from men. Even at Ceann Gronna in the past few years she had had to be careful. What was new was her own reaction to it, the pull of hardness on her nipples, her lack of breath as he watched her with eyes the colour of moss in a fast-running mountain stream. Even hating him, Isobel felt her body still drawn to his touch.

He had not hurt her. He had slept on the floor. He had given her water when she had asked and she had heard him instruct his men as he left to let no one in or out.

Protection.

A heady thing in circumstances such as her own.

Placing her head against the heavy wood of her

door, she listened. Voices could be heard on the other side. Guards that Marc had stationed there. Safety for now, at least. She breathed out in relief as she crossed to the bed, bringing the covers over her like a tent to keep out the cold.

Visions of Andrew falling into death plagued her, as did Ian's screams when the sword had passed through his stomach. She had no notion as to what had happened to anyone else. All lost. Eighty men and women gone in the blink of an eye under a force too strong to withstand. She should have sent them all away and stood on the battlements alone until she could do so no longer. She should have burnt what was valuable in the castle herself weeks before, once she knew of the large force coming from Edinburgh. So many other alternatives better than the one she had chosen!

She had failed and now she, too, would die. Perhaps to die slowly would be a just punishment for all the lives she had lost in her quest to protect the keep that was Dalceann. Her father's daughter, after all, and as greedy as he had been.

The sorrow that rose up in the back of her throat had her turning to the pillow to muffle heavy sobs of grief.

Voices woke her in the early afternoon, loud and angry just outside her door. There was the sound of thumping and of swordplay, the portal shaking as someone rammed against it.

Scrambling up, Isobel looked wildly around for furniture to shove in front of the door, finding it in an oversized chest on the far side of the room. With difficulty she got her shoulders behind the piece and shifted it with her body until it was stationed like a sentinel.

More shouting came from without and then a knock. Squeezing down on the urge to answer, she remained quiet. If it was Marc, he would have simply come in. The ropes at her wrist bit into her skin as she desperately tried to pry them loose.

'Lady Dalceann?'

A voice she did not recognise. She remained mute, counting the seconds between now and what would happen next.

The axe surprised her, splintering through the wood of her door again and again, small chips of oak hitting the ceiling.

Moving backwards, she grabbed a turned leg of the stool she had smashed yesterday by bending down on to her knees. With a weapon she felt better; it did not matter how useless she would be in wielding it with her hands tied behind her.

The heavy slats on this side of the door were still holding, but it could not be long until they were gone, too.

'What is it you want?' Her question had the effect of making the attack stop; a call for silence was heard through a widening hole. Perhaps it would buy her some moments.

Where was Marc de Courtenay? Why did he not come?

'We wish to talk to you.'

'About what?' There was not one tremor of fright in her words.

'The Dalceann soldiers in the dungeon—do you want them dead or alive?'

A different tack. Far more dangerous.

'Who are you? Give me your name.' Only anger marked her voice now, as she fought down the image of the death of the rest of her clan. By her reckoning she had about two minutes left before the door caved in. Walking to the window, she looked down. Sixty feet below her the inner courtyard sat—a quick death as opposed to a slow one and enough time to simply lean back hard and crash through.

Placing her right elbow against the wood, she tested it, for the axe was hammering at the door again and there was more shouting.

Now! She needed to lean into it right now, before they came in, before she was killed in a way she would have no say in, bit by bit, until life left her.

The main strap of wood gave way, rain coming on to her face. Nothing now between her and the afterlife save letting go. She opened her mouth to the water and let it fall upon her tongue, the small act of finding succour drawing her back from the abyss. Too late!

As the last resistance of the door fell away those on the other side were through. When she turned, she saw five soldiers opposite, all staring at her.

The man in the front was small and wiry and he carried a knife in his left hand.

'Lady Dalceann, you are indeed a beauty. No wonder de Courtenay had no wish to share.' He spoke gently, the words belying the meaning, but her eyes stripped away his smile.

'Come closer and I will jump.' No second thoughts this time. A quick death as opposed to a slow one.

The heavy leather strap of a horse whip snaked out and caught her leg, pulling her over. With her lack of balance she went down hard, stars showing in her vision.

They were on her before she had the chance to try to rise, ripping at the cotton of her kirtle and then at the ties of her chemise.

She bit out at a hand that passed by her mouth, sinking her teeth into a dirty palm and was rewarded with a smack across her face. The sharp blade of a knife cut away her hose and the air was suddenly cold against her bottom. Hands forced her legs apart, nails scraping at the skin.

No chance at all.

As she writhed to try to free herself, the small man unlaced himself, his intentions easy to see in the hard reddened ridge of flesh that sprang forwards.

With one last effort she screamed, but even that

was muffled, a wedge of material stuffed into her mouth and her hair gathered tight as she was pulled by the length of it backwards to her bed.

Marc had spent the early part of the afternoon outside, helping to move the bodies of the soldiers who had fallen in the battle, ferrying them to a barn that had not been razed near to where the tents were erected. He was wet and tired, the faces of fallen boys leaving him in a sour mood at the sheer waste of it all. Lord, his life had been for ever one of death and war. How many times had he said a prayer over the breast of those lost in battle? How many more times would he? He felt every single one of his twenty-nine years as he walked up the path to Ceann Gronna through the rain that had not eased.

Raised and angry voices alerted him to the fact that something was wrong as he started up the spiral staircase; realising it seemed to be coming from the vicinity of Isobel Dalceann's room, he began to run.

Drawing his sword, he pushed ahead, the hoarse scream of a woman floating above chatter.

Her door hung off its hinges, shards of wood littering the corridor. To the side his lieutenant lay, a bloodied cut to the temple. One of his men kneeled to give him aid and the other three were involved in a fight further down the corridor with the minions of Huntworth.

In the room Marc saw Archibald McQuarry and

his cronies around the bed in various states of undress. Isobel Dalceann lay alone, splayed out upon the mattress, a bruise beneath her eye and her clothes gone. The remains of her chemise had been pushed into her mouth, her hands still tied. Her bottom lip was swollen and bleeding and the marks of redness on her naked white shoulders told him just how rough they had been in getting her to the bed. White-hot fury consumed him.

'What the hell are you doing, McQuarry?'

'The same thing you did last night I presume, de Courtenay. Taking my pleasure with the spoils of war.'

'I am not finished with her yet.'

'Then get in line.'

'Oh, I think not.'

In one move he pushed the chest over on its edge so that it blocked the door-well, a dark wedge against any entry.

Five men. McQuarry was easy. His sword danced across the earl's skinny throat before he had the chance to speak and he crumpled to the floor, the vestiges of his sexual yearnings grotesque in the moment of his death.

The big man with the axe was next, parrying with it and then lunging. Marc felt the thrust of the blade against steel, but it was a primitive weapon with little finesse and before the man had the time to bring it back up it was too late. He joined his master on the floor.

Three men left now, with their blades drawn. As Marc moved away from the bed so that they might follow him, his glance caught Isobel scrambling up from her prone position, eyes all hollowed fear.

The sound of blades meeting rang out, but the corner was at his back now, sheltering him from being surrounded.

Ten thousand times he had done this dance. Thrust, withdraw, parry, feint. Old knowledge. An easy conquest.

Within a moment there was silence.

Laying his sword down, he broke the last of the wood lacings on the window and looked out to the gathering crowd below. Thankfully some of his own men stood amongst them.

'Tell the Lord of Glencoe that the Earl of Huntworth is dead,' he shouted, raising the axe against the weather, 'and tell him that I am now in charge of this keep.'

Spying one of his other lieutenants, he threw the hatchet and watched it spin in the descent, a harbinger of intent. 'Mariner, collect the weapons of any who might disobey and then bring a group you trust to my door. Those of you who take orders from me shall be rewarded well, I swear this on the name of King David the Second, for he has given me the sovereignty of his demands. Huntworth has tried to breach our king's favour by stealing that which was not his own and he has paid the price for such a betrayal.'

Reaching down, he hoisted his blade. 'Those with me, raise your swords.' A cheer came up as all hands came aloft. 'And those against me?'

Silence.

For the first time in ten minutes Marc took a breath that wasn't tight and forced as he turned to Isobel.

'I will not hurt you.'

When she nodded, he moved forwards to take the wad of material from her mouth, waiting until she took large gulps of air, panting with fright, the sound hoarse and shaken.

'Turn around.'

She did that also, her back to him now, the few tattered strips of her attire hiding nothing. When he sliced the bindings at her wrist she stretched out her arms. The ugly welts of red on her skin flared in the new-found freedom, the line of her spine straight beneath a heavy curtain of night-dark hair.

He would have liked to reach out and bring her to him in comfort, but now was neither the time nor the place and danger still lurked everywhere. Instead he lifted the blanket up from the floor on the dull side of his blade and placed it into waiting arms.

'Cover yourself,' he growled as voices from without became louder and he could hear the calls of his own men, 'and get behind me, for we are not safe yet.'

* * *

She was still alive and the awful certainty of what she thought might have happened, had not. Swallowing, Isobel again tasted blood on her tongue from her bottom lip. From one of the times that the man named McQuarry had lashed out, she supposed, and was glad the blanket was wide and thick and warm.

With Marc in the room fright and fear receded a little, though she held on to the end of the bed because, for a moment, everything spun at a dizzying angle.

'Don't you damn well faint on me.'

Looking up, she saw him watching her.

'I will not.' Chagrin replaced weakness and she stood to her full height.

'Good. Get the knife in the corner and hide it under your blanket. If anyone comes at you, kill them.'

'Even one of your own men?'

'Anyone!'

Swallowing, she understood exactly what such an answer must mean for him. Their glances caught, across the space of a small room, the blood in the wound near his ear changing the dirty blond of his hair to a soft pink, though he turned away when the chest in the door well began to move.

Men streamed into the chamber. All carried swords. The first man bent his head in a mark of respect and began to speak.

'Glencoe waits for you in the Great Hall, my lord. He said that he gives you his allegiance with that of his men.'

'And the soldiers of Huntworth?'

'Some have left for Edinburgh. Others wait for your orders. He was never a popular leader.'

'Good.'

'My men are cleaning out McQuarry's room as we speak. It still has a functioning door.'

'Then Lady Dalceann and I will retire there immediately, if you will show me the way.'

The big man nodded and stood back for them to pass as Marc drew his arm against her own and led her out, sword unsheathed.

'Bring the chest,' he ordered the youngest soldier, pointing to her cache of clothing.

They climbed the staircase to her mother's chamber, a room that had seldom been inhabited since she had left.

Large bundles of weaponry were stacked outside the portal. McQuarry's, she supposed, and tried not to look at them.

As they went in Marc replaced the slats behind those departing and then leant back against the wood, closing his eyes. Light from the window caught the blade at his side, throwing rainbows across the vaulted ceiling. Red, purple, yellow and blue. She counted the colours as he stayed silent, deep breaths marking the rise and fall of his chest. His exhaustion was so palpable it prompted her to speak.

'Thank you for your help.'

His eyes snapped open at her words. 'The oath in blood we took in the clearing below Kirkcaldy works both ways.'

The tone he used kept her mute as she digested his statement. His words were true. They were enemies sworn to protect each other. Such an impasse shimmered between them.

'In Edinburgh there is a handsome reward on your head and every man here would like to claim it. It would be best to remember that.'

'Every man including you?' His anger ignited hers, for there was only a certain amount of subservience that she could stomach.

Before he turned away she saw the truth in his eyes. Including him! Hurt unbalanced her.

'If the reward is to be paid in gold, I think you have already been well enough compensated.'

'You speak of the treasure hidden in your room, no doubt?' He waited till she nodded before continuing, 'It is in my safe keeping only because greed has the habit of tarnishing morality and is a useful tool when paying men to look the other way. You may well need such inducements to survive.'

'With that attitude it is no wonder that David's throne is weak.'

'Strong enough to take Ceann Gronna, Lady Dalceann.'

'Only because of your duplicity.'

His fingers came around her wrist like a vice. 'Unwise words can be as dangerous as the sharp point of a sword in the company of those who would take umbrage.'

'What would be the right ones, then?'

'Gratitude and acquiescence!'

'Death might be easier.'

He swore in French. 'You think with a face like yours that men will not scramble for the opiate of lust? Do you not understand that the curves of your body could so very easily assuage the lack of comfort many feel here far from their homes? Lord, do you truly imagine that a woman long lauded as the nemesis of David's commanders should be left to dictate the rules for her confinement under a triumphant army?'

'An army of bullies. Ceann Gronna has been sacked and the clansmen who I have lived with all my life are either dead or prisoners. Why should I now believe that you might protect me?'

'Because I just have.'

He let go of her as if her skin were aflame and she tried to get her breath to calm. Nothing made sense any more. She wanted to hurt him and she wanted to hold him. Only the distance of a foot kept them apart, a tiny space between what they were saying and what simmered beneath. Her body burned under the blanket for a gentle touch of skin that might take away fright and hate and meld it into something far more potent.

'I would see you safe, Lady Dalceann. At least believe that.'

His words were honestly said, without artifice or falsity; a man at the very end of his patience, yet still allowing her the mantle of his protection, no matter what it might cost him personally.

His admission doused anger and ignited the more familiar need that she had always felt in his company. Marc set something inside her on fire in a way Alisdair never had; she was torn again by the promise of eternal love she had given her dying husband and the warm and living knowledge of the one who had just saved her.

'Do you have a wife?'

The question made him frown, though he shook his head.

'I had a husband once who loved me. Alisdair. His name was Alisdair.' She wanted to say it suddenly and have the truth of goodness stated. 'He was my second cousin and a fine man. I thought our marriage would last for ever.'

She swallowed because even those words, those honest words, would not dull the ache of need that was beginning to fill her, despite everything that had just happened. She had been a good and dutiful wife when she had been married to Alisdair, but life went on and she was doing her best to survive it.

'I do not wish for that again, you understand. It is not love I seek tonight.'

'What is it, then, that you seek?' His stillness was intensified by the dust motes swirling in the air around him, caught in the last low light of the afternoon.

'I want to be held so close that the demons racing in my head are forced out. I want to be touched with care and honour and protection. And a shared need,' she added as the fire in his eyes flared bright. She wanted truth and integrity and honesty. She wanted the strength of him encircling fear, an enemy still, but a man who had fought his way through the worst of his own soldiers to rescue her.

'I want this.' Opening her fingers, she simply let the blanket go and stood still, cold air the only thing that covered her naked body.

Chapter Ten

She knew he saw the gouged trails of unwanted hands on the skin beneath, leading to the soft parts of her womanhood. For a second she thought he would turn away as fury darkened his eyes, but he did not, and the growing silence held in it a terrible understanding.

Alive. Still. After almost being raped. She shook away memory and latched on to another exactness.

Now. Here. With him.

An offering of herself to banish all the knowledge of what had so very nearly been.

Peeling away the last remains of her chemise, she let it fall from her fingers, so that nothing was hidden. Her nipples stood proud of their own accord, pushing towards him.

'I have never held to the notion of the rape of prisoners.'

'It is not rape that I am offering.' Her right hand cupped her left breast and she fondled it, her thumb running in circles across the hardening bud of nipple. With triumph she saw the rise of his manhood and the line of his jaw rippling under pressure. 'But the power of sex has a special forgetfulness and it is that I ask of you tonight. To forget what has just been... what might have happened if you had not come, just you against everyone.'

When he still did not move, she decided to tell him all of it. 'I dreamt of you after you left here, Marc de Courtenay. I wondered in the darkness what it would be like to touch you and have you touch me back. Sometimes in the early hours of another dawn when I did not sleep I imagined just this.'

She saw the moment restraint broke in the bruised greenness of his eyes burning with appetite.

Placing his sword down, he moved forwards and his hand covered hers. The heat of his skin seared away coldness. She was tall but he was taller. For the first time in her whole life she had to raise her chin to look up to a man and when his forefinger ran along the length of the scar on her cheek shock took away her breath.

'Tell me who hurt you.'

His tone disarmed her. So few had ever mentioned her affliction and none had touched her face where the sword had sliced the flesh in half.

Should she say what she had never told a soul before? Should she let him understand that it was not only politics that had led to the sacking of the keep, but also plain bare greed? Aye, and gold made fools of avaricious men.

'It was my father. The gold came from a French ship that sank off the rocks a few miles west of the cove at Ceann Gronna and he thought to keep it for himself.'

'To fight the king?'

'Nay. To disappear without a trace. When we tried to stop him, he turned on us. If we were dead, no one else would need to know.'

'What happened then?'

'Ian broke his neck and threw him into the sea at the mouth of a cave near Kincraig Point. But my father's arrow had already fatally pierced my husband.'

'God, Isobel.'

She shook her head, trying hard for indifference. 'Do not pity me. It is indeed the last thing that I should want from you.'

Unexpectedly he smiled and she felt the warmth of his touch move down to her breast, pushing away her grip so that his fingers might lie against the fullness instead. A warrior's hand, calloused and heavy. When he flicked his thumb across the sensitive skin she took in a breath and held it, thin pains of need piercing everywhere.

What now?

What came next?

The whole of her world was centred on the touch between them, the glory of sex bringing her forwards.

Not easy. Not soft or gentle. She did not want those things after all that had happened. She wanted elemental and carnal. She wanted to feel so much that there would be no space left for the fear that had engulfed her on the bed in her room as the fingers of her enemies had probed, seeking that which she had not wanted to give.

Her anger broke into a sob, unexpected and raw, hands gripping muscled forearms, nails leaving red crescents in the brown skin.

Hate and fear had such a surprising strength!

'Take me now, Marc. Make me forget,' she whispered, the deep longing of lust consuming her, like an opiate to memory.

Lord, help him. Isobel undressed was the most beautiful woman he had ever had the pleasure to look upon. His cock rose quickly, throbbing with the promise of what was offered.

Only lust.

She had made certain he had the knowledge of it. His engorgement grew tighter, strangling every reason as to why he should not do this, should not take her at her word and stop this thing between them that made nonsense of every promise he had given to himself.

But he could not! The heat of her skin drew him in as his head fell to her nipple and his lips fastened tight around the dusky pink. He heard the sound of blood in his ears and the moan of her need as she stretched back and brought her hands behind his nape to keep him anchored.

Home. On Isobel.

The taste of her centre, the swell of flesh, the musk of sex and abandon, no limits set. He shuddered as she pulled on his hair in the fury of her want, her legs straddling around his own, asking for other things, too, and not kindly.

Raising his head, he saw that her eyes up close were clear and rich with desire.

'I would never hurt you.'

'I know,' she whispered back, her tongue wetting her lips and her mouth opening as they came together hard, the force unstoppable and shocking.

He had spent a lifetime in control with women, always holding back things that he did not care to give despite their pleadings. But here, now, nothing was hidden or masked, no hesitation in any of it as his lips slanted against hers.

Power sliced through, white hot and unbridled, the room falling away into only sensation: her smell, her feel, her touch inside his ear, the promise of her mouth on his. Nothing made sense, balanced in this upper room above soldiers who would like to see his blood run freely across the courtyard flagstones.

He should be wielding his sword close with nothing to distract him. Instead he was brandishing another weapon, the hot stiffness of his manhood between them, the ache of release bound into a thin and unrelenting desperation.

His hands came around her bottom. He felt the long red weals of scratches on her skin.

Take me now, she had said, and he meant to.

Take me hard, she had implied, and his mouth marked her as his.

He lifted her easily, laying her on the bed covered in pelts sewn together. Her skin was white, luminescent against the sable of animal hide, the blue veins across her stomach inciting him into further emotion. When her legs fell open before him the particular scent of union beckoned him closer.

He looked nothing like Alisdair as he removed his hose and his sex sprung outwards. Her husband had been a small man and thin, his penchant for lovemaking uncertain even at the best of times. She could not even remember a night that he had truly wanted her, preferring instead to suckle at her breast until the skin around her nipple hurt with his insistence.

Sometimes when she could persuade him to enjoy more, he preferred the task completed as soon as possible, turning her so that she could not see him and dousing all the candles in the process.

He had never once looked at her as Marc did now, with greed and admiration in his eyes and the afternoon light strong across the room. When he wet his finger with spit and drew it across her nipple she felt the sharp slip of a desire that was fathomless.

His thighs were heavily muscled and sprinkled with dark hair. Reaching out, she touched him, feeling the planes of strength until he swore and guided her fingers to his shaft of red. His own hands surrounded hers, holding her there in a quiet pressure, smooth stretched skin expanding in her hand.

Not all taking, then, but giving. She liked the vulnerability of him and the easy knowledge of how very much he desired her drawn into the heavy throb of flesh.

Shifting forwards she guided the tip of him into her mouth and heard him swear. His hands fell slack and she took him deeper, laving her tongue and closing her eyes so that she might just simply feel, him in her, at her mercy, centred in touch.

So very easy to make a man her own, the shattered breath as his chest rose quick to match her rhythm and he threw back his head and groaned.

She had never done this before, never brought a man to coitus with her mouth, though in her bed at night after Alisdair had finished his quick ministrations she had dreamed of it. Tasting.

He pulled away even as she thought he might come, might leave the white milk of his surrender inside her, to savour and remember when he was gone.

'God.' His voice was rough. 'God,' repeated again as he ran one hand through his hair, the hint of distrust shadowing both eyes into the very darkest of green.

Uncertainty.

She could not care that she saw things she did not wish to in his face. Nothing was important save a release from that which kept her stiff and tense, the ache in her body focused now around the muscles between her legs. She wanted him there, wanted him to wipe away the terror of before, the impotence and the weakness. She needed her power back, strong and certain, giving what she wanted and to whom she wanted to, melding the mastery of sex into an authority of her will.

'Please.' She meant not to say it even as she did, tipping her head back and raising her hips. Her fingers dug into the mattress like talons.

If he leaves now I shall hate him!

But he did not go, the quiet whisper of words comforting when he bent to the contour of her waist and then her hips. His right hand bundled the length of her hair and bound it in a fist, tethering them together.

She could not pull away. This was exactly what she craved: mastery and skill. No hurt in it but no pity, either, just the feel of a male against her and his intentions plainly given.

'The battle for Ceann Gronna went as God willed it, Isobel, but perhaps in the spoils afterwards other things can be salvaged, aye?'

'Things like this.' She hardly recognised her voice, hoarse with longing, and she writhed as his fingers fell into the folds between her legs, skirting inwards.

'Marc?' His name as a question in the midst of all that had been and her thighs open so that he might find the path that the others had not quite discovered and wipe away the terror.

'Look at me,' he said suddenly, 'and tell me that this is what you want from me.'

His eyes showed the whites, like a stag in full roar, she thought. Such greed made him magnificent, a warrior and a knight who would be hers on the turn of one tiny word.

'Yes.'

Her whole body shook as she moaned it, the pain of waiting more than she could bear.

Neither anger nor hate. Not hurt or desperate loathing, but a cleansing. She closed her eyes as one finger found its way inside, stretching her, while another rested on a nub that made her buck up with the very perfectness of it.

Lord, what was he doing? How did he know of this? His rhythm heightened and it took her body, up and up into a realm where nothing was left save the quest for what he promised, this magician warrior, inside her as she exploded into warm languid waves of feeling.

Pulsating and shaking, he took all her will as he

played the sweet final shades of music, the clenching in her abdomen repeated in her very toes.

Then stillness and a bitter sweet echo of pain.

Tears fell from her eyes, but she neither wiped them away nor opened them. She did not want to see him yet or wish for the world to intrude on the perfect.

This was her secret and one she had never before discovered about herself. Such a gift. It was barely comprehensible.

She felt him move, of course, off the bed and towards the door. Away from her. She watched him under hooded lids trying to understand his feelings, but his face was set as he pulled on his hose and repositioned his armoury.

She had not pleased him. She had not taken him inside her and let him ride until he was replete and the demons that hounded a man were quiet. Alisdair had told her of it once, when she had asked him of his proclivity for her breasts rather than the womanhood between her legs. Demons took those who used the sin of lust as a balm, he had explained, and impure thoughts were not to be encouraged.

Her hand ran across the swell of her stomach and then down to the wetness between her legs.

She had never felt such a thing before. Lord, was she like those loose women of the night? Had Marc thought her such and would leave because of it? Even now not five minutes after the last wave of pleasure she craved him again, weaving the magic of his fingers on the hardened bud of her femininity.

The bang of the door had her turning into the soft pillow to block out the empty room.

His anger spiralled into cold wrath as he stalked along the corridor to the outside ramparts.

He needed air and chill to douse the fierce want that had consumed him, that had broken through his normal control and left him coveting things that would never come to pass.

A family.

A wife that he could grow old with.

A home that was not sacked by battle and a monarch who might reward him with quiet retirement into peace.

He was Sir Marc de Courtenay, the first commander of kings who dealt in the realm of the fine gains of war. He was a bastard in two courts and a man who knew enough secrets about them both to destroy nations.

He had no hope for what he dreamed of, no earthly prospect of armistice and serenity, no knowledge of home or hearth or family. All these things had long been taken from him—at birth when his mother had failed to survive her confinement and then later when he had been sent down as an apprentice to a man who thought nothing of beating a child until his skin bled with it.

War and battle had given him back his place, at the front of soldiers who would do whatever it was he asked of them even in the moments of utter rampage. Charge and attack was a death very often only thinly disguised by his orders.

His right hand sat on its own accord across the hilt of his sword at the ready. Another habit.

His fingers remembered the soft folds inside Isobel and the wetness that had spilt across his fingers when she had found her final oblivion. He brought the hand to his nostrils, capturing what essence was still left there, tasting it again in the quiet cold stone of the corridor.

He could have stayed, but her orgasm had brought him shame and discomfort. Did she cry out for another loss, less brutish than McQuarry's attempts at subduing her, but every bit as effective?

He remembered her silence and her vulnerability, and all the other things that Isobel Dalceann had never been before Ceann Gronna had fallen.

Defeated. Taken. Subdued. Vanquished.

The tears on her right cheek had magnified the place where even her own father had tried to kill her.

He should not have plucked the centre of lust from her with such little abandon. He should have tucked her into bed with her fright and left her there to rise in the morning without a great temptation to hate him for the exposed uncertainty that she had let him see.

A hot-blooded woman was Isobel Dalceann, with

her generous breasts and tight quim and legs finer and longer than any woman he had found oblivion with.

Faceless women, now that he had seen her. He shook his head. There it was again, this spell that lingered in her ability to make a man mad with want. He leaned back against the wall and toyed with the idea of just going back and taking, for his own sake now, no kindness in it save the hope that she would be gone from his mind come the morrow.

Aye, the unbalance of sex seduced him with possibility. She could be beneath him in less than a full minute, writhing wet as he emptied himself of a tension that brought the blood into his temples. She even wanted it, for God's sake. Sweat beaded his upper lip and made him dizzy with avidity. His manhood, still stiff in his hose, showed no signs of abating and he was sick of the effort it took to stay where he was and not turn back.

Isobel. Under him. Her eyes golden with lust and acquiescence. Her breasts tipped hard and thrusting as he escorted her with his erection to the same place his hands had just managed to.

So very easily! But he could not destroy any more of her.

His breath quickened and, striding towards the Great Hall, he resolved to drink his fill of the fine whisky brought up in kegs from the Ceann Gronna cellars.

Chapter Eleven

She wore a kirtle of blue and a bliaud of grey, the colour of sadness, when he went to her room the next morning, and around her waist she had fashioned prayer beads. Her hair was hidden under a barbet and veil, whilst on her feet she favoured soft boots of leather.

Like a novice almost, or a virtuous young maid in the first blush of youth with the mantle of religion firmly draped around her. In spite of everything Marc smiled because no one else in his entire life had managed to confound him as Isobel Dalceann did.

He saw piety in her stance and in the way she bowed her head, a frown on her forehead and her teeth worrying her swollen bottom lip.

All the small gestures were exactly right; he could not have faulted such a performance even as he wondered where it was she had secreted the knife he had given her.

'Breakfast will be sent up. I thought it prudent to keep you out of sight for this morning at least.'

She stood before the window, a few small wisps of dark hair escaping around the edges of the fabric tied beneath her chin. The dawn burnished everything, lending the room a repose that had not been there the afternoon before.

'Thank you.'

She did not raise her eyes to meet his, but kept them downcast.

Disquiet began to fill him.

'I hope you slept well.'

The only sign of anything being amiss was the tightening of her fingers on the cloth of her bliaud.

'Very well.'

His own ire rose at such an answer. He had spent most of the night trying to drink himself into a stupor and failing.

But looking at her more closely, Marc saw that the circles beneath her eyes were dark and the bruise on her cheek where she'd been hit by the bastard McQuarry had turned purple.

He also saw that the silver ring she wore on her marriage finger was missing. Little details, but important. Women seldom did things on a whim, he had come to understand in his life of knowing many, and although other men laughed at the capriciousness of the feminine sex he himself had never found that to be true.

Nay, women only did things after much reasoning and debate.

'The castle is safe for you now, Lady Dalceann. No one shall dare place a hand upon your person.'

That brought her glance up. She was angry. He could see it in the shifts of muscle on her face and in the puckering of her scar. The brown in her eyes was almost black.

'What will happen to me, then?' There was a cadence in her voice that he had not heard there before—beyond caring, if he could have named it.

'You will be taken to Edinburgh to stand before the king.'

'I see.' She did not even flinch at the words. 'And my men?'

'Will remain here until the fate of the keep is properly resolved.'

'Properly.' She echoed the word and her bosom strained against dove-grey material. He made his eyes come away from the roundness, almost embarrassed when she saw where it was he looked. The cross on a pin at her waist caught the new day, like a warning from a deity who understood the more shameful wants of men.

Would he ever be able to see her and not want her? Would he ever forget what she had looked like under the candlelight, writhing in ecstasy as his fingers lay deep within her?

He turned away.

'King David will kill me.'

He turned back. 'No. He will give you pardon and allow you safe harbour amongst his court.'

Because I shall insist on it as the boon I was promised before setting out into Fife. Such a thought overrode all others. He would not see one hair on her head harmed, he swore it.

'The gold will help with such a sanctuary.'

'You forget, my lord, the treasure is no longer in my care.'

'For this time mayhap not, but when you have the need of it, it will be returned.'

'I see.'

He thought her chin wobbled for a second, but there was no certainty in such a deduction because a knock on the door brought them both into action.

She darted behind him, the dirk he had wondered about in her hand and full drawn whilst he remained still, the bulk of his body shielding her from any threat that might materialise.

'Who knocks?'

'Mariner. There is an emissary from the king who has just arrived at the gate. Glencoe thought you might wish to meet him together.'

'I shall come immediately.'

When he looked back at her the knife was gone, the pious version of the beautiful Lady Dalceann again in place. He was pleased to see a serving woman bring in a plate of bread and meats and a jug of mead as he went.

* * *

She listened to him go, his steps disappearing one by one and taking him from her into the company of a messenger who might have brought her death warrant.

The pardon was a ruse, an empty promise of nothingness. So many of those in her life. Her father. Alisdair. The king. Her mother. And now him.

After her shame of the previous night there would be no more honesty between them. She was sure of it. No woman of birth would have ever lain as she did with his hands between her thighs held tight by the muscles of her lust or his staff full in her mouth in the way of a baby suckling at the breast of its mother.

He thought her a whore every bit as unchaste as those who sold themselves in numerous market towns up and down the coast for a penny or a crust of bread. Desperate women with bairns to feed and the swelling presence of another inside them.

Such was the fate of women. In that she should be glad that he had not entered her and left his seed to take before throwing her to the mercy of an ungodly king.

She wrung her hands as the shouts of the newcomer's welcome could be heard in the lower bailey, the pale skin that had once lain beneath her wedding ring catching her notice.

Gone.

Alisdair would not recognise the woman that she

had become and so she had removed it. She was glad that Ian or Angus or Andrew were not here in the room to see her, either, for her desire for Marc de Courtenay was only thinly disguised by anger. It would not take much to make her beg him again for what she had enjoyed last night.

Even the thought had her pacing, a woman lost from sense. He would sacrifice her to the king and still she would want him?

Shaking her head hard, she picked up a crust of bread. Lord, she had barely eaten in days and the warm dough was fresh and tasty. Adding the meat to it, she finished the morsel quickly before starting on another.

She was alive and she was well fed. She had experienced the joy of lovemaking with a man who was both gentle and adept at pleasuring a woman. Her men were secure for the moment in the basement dungeons and Ceann Gronna keep still stood, proudly as it had done for a hundred years, and Marc had promised the remaining women would be safe from rape.

Not all was lost, then. Now it was up to her to turn the situation in which she found herself into one that was tenable. An idea began to form, crystallising beneath thought.

Men were slaves to sensation and Marc de Courtenay would be no different. Perhaps if she played her cards with dexterity, protection might follow. He had, after all, already offered a show of it; dressed in these woman's clothes, it would be far easier for her to act out the part required. If she promised him the use of her body when and where he should want it, would he be amenable to allowing her last soldiers the chance to slip away unnoticed?

Perhaps he might say they had perished or were ransomed, the gold he held ample for such a pledge.

Her fingers ran across the line of her bodice and she smiled, feeling the old power running back into her. Nay, the war was not lost at all and with a full stomach and a new resolution she walked to the window to stare down on to the ramparts of the baileys, now being patrolled by the king's men.

Desperate situations required desperate measures, she told herself, even as anticipation mounted. She was neither young nor a virgin; if men could meet in battle and sacrifice their bodies, then so could women.

But when to start?

Tonight. The answer came quickly. He would not be expecting it and his guard would be down. This time, however, it would not be merely her pleasure that would be attended to because, if this whole idea was going to work, she needed Marc de Courtenay to want her as he had never craved another.

The very thought brought heat into her cheeks and she fanned away the warmth. Could she do it? Could she play the siren with such conviction that he might not question her motives?

Yes. Running her thumb down a sheet of polished

horn sitting against the mantel, she felt the innate and surging capability of womanhood and was fortified again when her reflection gave no sign at all of the disfiguring scar.

Marc resisted going back up the stairs to the chamber of Isobel Dalceann until the light of the day began to fade and he knew that to do any different might incite questions.

For the first time in all his life he felt...uncertain. Even then realisation of such an emotion astonished him.

The emissary from the king had been most definite. He was to bring the Lady of Ceann Gronna immediately back to Edinburgh to face the consequences of revolt and he was experienced enough to know that a monarch under pressure would not treat a rebellious citizen lightly.

Not even one with the face of an angel.

Isobel might have been right, after all, when she had said that to go to Edinburgh could only result in her death. The options closed in on him. To protect her he would have to expose himself and, although he had allies in the royal court of Scotland, he doubted that it would be enough. In France it would have been different.

Glencoe had been present at today's discussions, David's man through and through, and it seemed that they would start out for Edinburgh from Ceann

Gronna on the morrow. The king had sent more of his own soldiers as well, a further bolster to make certain that royal orders were followed to the letter, and they watched the castle carefully.

Aye, the price of war and dissension could be paid for dearly in blood by the daughter of a man who had not possessed the wisdom to see where such intemperance might lead.

Standing outside their room he breathed in, knowing that Isobel Dalceann would be waiting to find out about today's visitors and weighing up the exact amount of truth he might give her.

He came in quietly, his sword left in the shelves beside the doorway, the hilt of it positioned in a way that he could retrieve it at the first sign of danger. She liked the sound of the key turning in the door behind him and the movement of feet outside as if they had been dismissed for the night to a place further off.

Privacy would serve her well.

Her bare feet felt the softer edge of a rug as she moved forwards. The green in his eyes sharpened the moment he registered how her clothing had changed from the morning. The grey in her bodice was opened to the warmth of a fire stoked in the hearth. She had made certain that the hint of soft linen beneath where the edge of breasts pushed against it could be seen. The barbet and veil had gone, too, her hair released around her shoulders and falling long down her back.

'I hope it went well today, my lord.'

A slight caution beneath careful control told her that it had not, even as he assured her it had.

'Are you hungry?'

When he nodded she gestured for him to sit and brought forwards a generous plate of chicken and pork accompanied by trenchers of freshly baked bread. She smiled when he looked up, just as a woman of good nature and easy disposition would have. She knew he could smell the attar of violets that she had applied liberally on all the bare parts of her skin because his nostrils flared when she leaned across him, her loosened hair falling forwards as she hoped it would. She had noticed other maids do that when they sought to attract a suitor—a quick flick of their hands through their tresses, inviting observation. Isobel only wished she could have washed it properly in the lavender water that the housekeeper at Ceann Gronna favoured, but only a small bowl of plain water had been delivered to her room.

Still, her awkward ministrations seemed to be doing something because Marc de Courtenay was watching her in exactly the same way he had yesterday, the interest on his face stamped with the unmistakable essence of masculine lust.

'I have been lonely in here all day by myself.'

Lord, was this overdoing it? A crease in his brow

told her that perhaps it was, so she tempered her next sentence. 'Though I expect that you have been very busy?'

Sometimes she had heard the maids talking in the kitchens of lovers when they had forgotten that she was there and they always stressed the importance of asking a man about his day and listening intently.

Again she flicked her fingers through her loosened braid, though this time he stopped her simply by raising his hand against her own and stilling it.

'I should not wish for falseness from you, Isobel.'

'Falseness?' She hated the way her voice rose of its own accord in a shrill intonation of a question.

'You seem a different woman tonight from the one I left this morning.'

'I have had the whole day to ponder the fate of Ceann Gronna and if the trials and tribulations of the king should come to rest on Dalceann shoulders, I doubt the outcome will be good.' Lord, she suddenly thought, talking politics was the very wrong way to go about seduction.

Trying to regroup, she sat on the stool opposite him and lifted the hem of her gown so that her ankles might be on full show.

'We leave for Edinburgh tomorrow.'

She hitched her skirt up further, pleased when his eyes took in the full line of her lower legs as she stretched them out under the pretence of a cramp. He stopped eating, the candlelight between them throwing a soft sheen across the room.

Tomorrow! So very little time!

'How long were you married for?' His question was asked with an edge of wariness.

'Two years and three months. Alisdair was killed just before the second campaign.'

The day she tried not to remember surrounded her, bitter-cold and noisy, the cry from the lips of her husband as he had died in her arms and the screams of her father as he paid the price of such betrayal.

A traitor came in many forms, after all. It was her fault that Alisdair had even been there in the first place as he had wanted to pray for guidance in the Ceann Gronna chapel, but she had insisted that he accompany her to confront her father down by the caves at Kincraig Point.

These were the things that she had told no one, these sins of hers, lost in the death of a husband whom she should have protected and had not.

Standing, she moved to the window, feeling the cold of the early summer in her bones.

The loosened bodice and the potent perfume seemed suddenly foolish and, rubbing her wrist against her skirt, she tried to erase some of the scent before bringing the lacings about her neck tighter. She was Isobel Dalceann, the chief of the clan of Dalceann, and the prime defender of her keep. There was no other choice but to act.

'If you can rescue Ceann Gronna's people from the wrath of King David, I swear I will sleep with you whenever and wherever you might want to, Marc de Courtenay.'

There. It was said. She looked at him directly, no artifice left under the truth as she had stated it. The anger in her made the very beat of her heart thrum in her ears. It was useless playing the flirt when every part of her rebelled at the thought.

When would this woman ever stop surprising him? The pulse in her throat was racing even as she caught his glance, challenging him to answer. The old Isobel was back in full force, her eyes flinting away the incredulity that he felt rising within.

She was magnificent in her nun-grey attire and her promise of easy favours, her hands at her side balled into tight fists should he refuse her offer.

Every single part of him rose to say yes and take her here in the high turreted room of the lime-washed Ceann Gronna Castle, but such forthright honesty needed care.

'I am a knight, Isobel, and David has sent me here to Fife under oath to serve him.'

'A king's man, then, without question?' There was anger in her voice, and also disappointment.

'Nay, more of a pragmatic one. If you do not come before the Edinburgh Court you will never be safe. Neither here in Scotland nor in the wider world, for the enemies of dissension are everywhere and well rewarded should they bag their quarry. Besides, if you fail to accompany us to stand before the king, I doubt your men would thank you for it.'

'The king would have them killed?'

He shrugged his shoulders, trying to imbue in the action some sense of his own bewilderment. 'He has the legal right to any action he might consider appropriate in the safeguarding of his throne and your keep is not the only one refusing to acknowledge the new feudal law. It is my guess that the wealthy barons from the north would also unseat him, given any stirring of weakness.'

Seeing her rising anger, he changed tack. 'Your father's poor judgement need not be reflected in yours, however, and it is wise in such adversity to at least tender a semblance of contrition. I am of the opinion that David will accept an earnest apology.'

'You see this as a game?' she returned. 'You offer me advice on the finer points of pretence on the one hand and swear undying allegiance to your monarch on the other? Where is the honour in that, I ask?'

'Here.' He gestured, swiping his fingers over the skin at his neck. 'My head still stands on my shoulders and I still breathe into another day.'

'With truth and justice sacrificed?'

His laughter filled the room. 'You think Ceann Gronna's defiance might change the way history is written if all within it lie dead? What of the fact that the Crown is anointed by God in its ownership of land?'

She shook her head, highlights of darkness caught in the candle above the mantel. 'A truth written in which Bible?'

'A royal one, I should imagine, and penned in the blood of those who might insist it otherwise.'

Her smile was fierce and momentary. 'A man who stands unhindered by law and in the shoes of Our Lord on earth is dangerous even to those who would support him.'

'God, Isobel.' For the first time Marc understood some of the things that were said of her in Edinburgh and the knowledge curdled his very blood. 'One word of this outside our room and you will be tried for treason. Even I could not save you.'

The sentiment echoed in a growing silence as they watched each other, the realisation of all they had said falling into a place that was new and changed. Marc had never spoken with one other person in the way that he had spoken with her—the truth of sedition versus the integrity of faith, faith to believe in dreams and to follow them. *Mon Dieu,* how many times had he lain there at night on yet another battlefield littered with the bodies of young and zealous men and ruminated on the fickleness of monarchs and their unwarranted omnipotence? Him, a king's man, and no choice in any of it save death.

Until now, here, with Isobel.

The heat he always felt between them flared, her skin soft beneath the material of her bliaud and the lace on her chemise finely crafted.

'The Dalceann name comes with its own costs. I grant you that.' He could not quite disguise his admiration.

'Then let me not be one of them.'

Lord, but she was good; the brown in her eyes melted into gold. He could hardly breathe with the memory of last night everywhere in the room.

Reaching out, he took her left hand into his and touched the skin at the base of her fourth finger. 'I cannot promise your freedom, Isobel, but I can promise you pleasure tonight.' Leaning down to run his tongue across the line of paleness on her marriage finger, he smiled when she did not pull away.

Chapter Twelve

Again.

She almost said it, her body rising to the promise.

Again and again and again.

Disquieting for your heart to wish for that which your head knew you should deny, but there it was, unstoppable and absolute. Her father's daughter, after all, with no reason behind actions that could only humiliate her given his stance on not violating the trust of his monarch.

'I should like that.'

She enjoyed his shocked stillness, this knight of kings and wars, with the signs of battle written on him in opaque-scarred tissue and a controlled distance that seldom showed any sort of emotion. She had seen him fight and knew that his skills in the art of warfare must be lauded from one edge of this world to the other, his swordplay unlike any she had ever had the pleasure to witness. The king's man he professed to be, but his own man, too. When he spoke of politics and court life, there was no mindless allegiance promised, but questions posed.

How had he been able to hide such intemperance in Burgundy and here?

Some part of the whole was missing, she thought, even as he ran his finger across her ear, distracting her. There was a truth that he was not saying beneath everything else that he was.

'Can you promise me something, Isobel, something that might be hard to fathom at this moment?'

The green in his eyes was close, the lashes that fringed them thick, and for a second she felt a fear that held no boundary.

She would lose him in Edinburgh to other ladies of pure breeding and good manners, lose him to women without ruined faces or fathers who would dare to question kings.

'Can you promise to trust me in Edinburgh even if you do not understand the reasons for my actions? Protection is a narrow path and if you should wander off it…' He stopped. 'I can only help you if you trust me.'

Such a gentle word, trust, and so easily broken. She had trusted in her father's guardianship and Alisdair's libido. She had trusted in her mother's love and in the innate good sense of law. She had trusted the walls of Ceann Gronna to withstand invasion across as many springs as she might live.

She saw that he was waiting for an answer.

'Andrew always said that Edinburgh is the place of lies. Is this trust that you would ask of me another of them?'

His fingers tightened around hers.

'Even a falsehood well executed might be enough to save you.'

'From David?'

He frowned at that as he gathered her into his arms. 'There is always more than one powerful man in any court, Isobel. Sometimes it is just a matter of finding him.'

'But you will help me do that?'

'You will help yourself by understanding that kings require very careful handling and that allegiance, fealty and loyalty are only words.'

'You sound seasoned in the art of such expedience.'

He did not answer as he moved up against her, her back flat against the warmth of a woollen tapestry in red and yellow and strands of the more luxurious purple.

'I want you, Lady Dalceann. I want all of you this time, but not as a pawn or a hostage to demand conditions from a king and not as the leader of the clan, either, who might think to save her men by offering her body in sacrifice.'

He pushed his groin against her stomach and she felt the rigid need in him. 'I want you tonight away from the war and the killing, lying with the moon upon your nakedness, spent with fervency.'

'Yes,' she whispered and the world stood still, the hours of dark between this moment and the morning filled with a promise that was exhilarating.

Liberty and pleasure—had she ever in her life felt the anticipation of both? And how fleeting would they be now?

The muscles in his arms rippled as he peeled back his tunic and the chiselled contours of his chest under her fingers were firm.

Beautiful. She hated the pull of such perfect symmetry, given the lack of it in her own face as she leaned her head down to take the skin of his shoulder between her teeth. He tasted of salt and woodsmoke and safety.

'When I pulled you from the sea I thought you were a god in your braided surcoat,' she confessed. 'And I wondered if you could be real.'

His fingers closed against her cheek, cradling her face. 'But now you know that I am.'

His other hand fell lower across the line of her bottom, invoking the same feelings as before, all the thoughts she had lain in bed and dreamed of, sleepless with prescience.

Her centre quickened, melting in the hope of repetition, his skin drawing her in until no space at all lay between them; the breath she held allowed her the stillness that she needed to simply perceive: his scent in her nostrils, his heartbeat slow and steady under her touch, his growing ardour in the hard outline of manhood beneath flimsy hose.

This was the heaven she had sought for so long, this silence of feeling with nothing distracting the twin pull of souls in their quest to recognise completion.

Elation bloomed and brought a flush to her face.

Was it possible this was more than lust, more than just a momentary union of flesh? Her eyes widened with the question because no words of more had ever fallen between them. All there had been was the choler of war.

She shook her head. She could not care. With a thousand days of battle behind and the chance of something wonderful ahead she took it, opening her thighs to his gentle fingers and arching her neck when he petitioned entry.

Her hair fell in a dark curtain around his arms, the shades in it of flame and sable and midnight as he found the warmth of her, slipping fingers into wetness with ease.

The sirens of Circe themselves had no purchase on Isobel's elemental sensuality. She was like fire and water in his arms, writhing with the pressure of him, her hips bucking as she rode his hand, beckoning him in further.

He swore because he could no longer contain that

which he had been trying to. A limited loving. The sweat on his brow and his lip beaded and the sense he had promised himself was lost. He could not deny her.

She would be his tonight.

Lifting her, he laid her legs on his thighs, positioning himself so that gravity brought her down upon him hard. He felt her sheath fold in around him, tight and wet, her eyes opening to his as the length drove inwards. Nothing held back as he buried himself to the hilt and then pulled away to do exactly the same again.

He could not stop, the feel of her slickness egging him on, the movement of her breasts against his chest, nipples tight with the intimacy. He wanted her until he was breathless and all the demons in him were at peace.

Nothing else existed save for Isobel, her cries hoarse as he drove in again and again, pushing further, relief rising until he reached up and simply seized it, panting with the quittance as he exploded into oblivion, spilling his seed.

He could not pull back, could not leave the promise, could not understand, either, what had just happened to him as the control he always protected slipped into chaos. His heart in his throat beat without rhythm or pattern as the words of gratitude rose.

'Thank you.' He could barely say them as they fell down upon the bed, curled into each other's warmth.

* * *

She closed her eyes and felt him there inside her still, the last echoes of muscle clenching him close, her body languid with the joy of sex.

The earth had moved. She remembered only three weeks ago, when the king's army had streamed on to the lands at Ceann Gronna, worrying that she might never know what it was she now did.

The imprint of him was stamped into her, the liquid from his body within her own. She wanted to hold and savour it, to know that a small piece of him brought the hope of a child, his child, conceived in a room after war.

'I should withdraw.' His words. The breath of them tickled the space on the top of her head.

'No.' She kept him immobile with the pressure of her thighs, bidding him to stay as cold air doused heat.

'If you do much more of that, I cannot be answerable to what might happen next, Isobel.'

His hand stilled her, lying across her thigh so that the deeply scarred part on his forearm was visible and the pad of her first finger reached out to touch. 'How did this happen?'

'I was a child without protection,' he returned and twisted, leaving it no longer in sight.

'There is much I do not know about you.'

He straightened, so that his clear green gaze fell upon her.

'Yet there is a lot, my love, that you do.' His smile made her insides coil into warmth. *My love?* Just a term he had used carelessly or a real endearment?

The masculine grace of him lying before her was so very enticing. She pushed against him and felt him grow within.

'Yes,' she said softly as he turned and came above, his elbows taking the weight of his body.

'Yes,' she repeated as he twisted the heaviness of her hair around his fist and held her captive.

No little loving. No half-hearted attempts. He simply watched her face taking the breadth of him, plunging in as far as he could go until she relaxed.

This was what her body had been made for, this abundance flowing into an ache of need, and when his hand found her nipple and ran across it in the same rhythm as his cock she let go of inhibition and cried out.

'Don't stop, Marc. Don't you dare stop.'

She began to shake as he lifted her hips, the nub that he fondled taking away rational thought and bringing her nails fully along the naked line of his back.

Her breath could not come as the waves of pleasure that bound her body to his exploded into a primitive need that held no sway to whispered messages of loving.

She just wanted him, inside her, anchored to desire and appetite. Her stomach swelled, the melting soft inside burgeoning outwards so that she went to pieces with the want, wave after wave clenched into breathlessness.

Afterwards, he slipped away from her when she let him, but his fingers came into the space he left, lying still, small harbingers of an unfinished loving, opening her thighs.

Fleshless and spent. If an enemy had broken through the door, she could not have raised even an eyelid. She waited to see what might come next in this lesson of a loving she had only ever dreamed of.

He should leave her now, for she had been tight and small and he knew more would have her bruised upon the morrow. But he could not make his body obey his head, as his cock ached for more, as he leaned over and took her nipple in his mouth, kneading the ample flesh beneath.

For this moment Isobel Dalceann was his. For this night on the wild coast of the Firth above Elie, the turrets of Ceann Gronna silhouetted against a sea that reached all the way to Europe, she was his conquest, willing and compliant. Jesus, he could not remember a time when he had taken a woman thrice in a row, but the heat in him had resurfaced and his fingers began to move.

He felt her breath against his skin, felt the way she turned to him, felt her hand reach down to his hardness and guide him in from behind.

Accepting.

He had her on her hands and knees within a second, the length of her hair falling to the fur in one long swathe and her breasts swinging heavy under his thrusts. This time he altered the tempo, fast and then slow, the uncertainty of his strokes purposeful, and she begged him to keep going when he withdrew, poised at her entrance.

God, she was wet, the moistness of her ran down his shaft, glistening, beckoning completion, and when she began to pant he emptied himself into the swollen pinkness and collapsed on top of her pinning her beneath him with no mind for his weight.

Just breath and sweat and the sweet scent of sex, filling the room around them in the particular way of lovers.

He wanted to stay here for ever, with her beneath him, the world at bay and a handful of long hours before the dawn.

Only Isobel.

Only her.

The muted shadows cast wide across the room as she lay pinned to the bed.

A teardrop welled in her right eye, pooling until it dropped down her cheek to be soaked up by the bolster beneath. This was what it felt like to be fully used by a man who understood the power of union. No half-measures or excuses. No easy gentleness, either. He had given her everything and taken everything.

Another tear followed the first one; to think that she might have limited such an act with her own motives of aiding her escape. The world turned on the moments between then and now. Then she did not understand the perfect beauty inherent in the game of mating and now she did.

He had shown her to herself, her cries unfettered by the pure joy of it all. She had never before felt her body take rein as it did with him, the wrenching bliss releasing all the tensions of so many days of siege. Even now with such a thought the echo of it ached in her bones.

When he rolled off she turned to face him, unwilling to let the bond between them go. Her fingers rose up to link with his, holding them together.

'My husband was not a man who enjoyed my body.'

He laughed at that and gripped her fingers tighter. 'He must have been a eunuch, then, to pass up the chance of loving you well.'

'I think he felt it was shameful to take pleasure in the marriage bed.' She had never told anyone that. She waited for his answer.

'Was he a good husband in other ways?'

'Yes.' A simple word and all the guilt dropped away. 'He was my friend.'

'Then you were lucky.'

The call of a guard on the western tower kept them quiet, listening for the answering shout. It came a few seconds later, a keep bedded down for the evening, all gates shut.

'What will happen to Ceann Gronna?'

'It will be passed on to one of the barons loyal to David for a sum that will help the royal coffers, I suspect.'

'No longer Dalceann, then?'

'Few families last for ever in their domains, Isobel. Be thankful the keep was not razed and the people here are still alive.'

'I am.' She rose up on her elbows and looked straight at him. 'I have you to thank for that, Marc.'

He shook his head. 'When you arrive in Edinburgh you may not thank me for much at all.'

'My father's stance was not your responsibility.'

'Maybe not. But your welfare is.'

'Because I am your captive?'

He laughed again. 'Much more than that, aye.'

His other hand threaded behind her neck and he brought her head down to his, finding her lips with only the lightest of pressure.

'Just this now,' he whispered as she went to speak, his tongue coming in against her own, tasting the essence. When she relaxed into his will he turned her beneath him and everything wonderful began all over again.

Chapter Thirteen

They had been travelling for three days and Isobel had barely seen Marc in all that time.

The king's men surrounded her, their livery different from that of the other soldiers, and the cart she travelled in was comfortable.

Margaret, one of the Ceann Gronna maids, had been brought on the journey as her companion, and she sat on the seat opposite, eyes wide open as she looked upon the scene through the gaps of leather draping the conveyance.

Hiding her from everyone? Isobel had not failed to notice the stares of men whose eyes raked the scar on her cheek as she was brought down into the Great Hall at Ceann Gronna.

Marc had been there with a group of soldiers by the fireplace and for the first time she saw him properly within the company of others. She swallowed back the difference. He watched her like a stranger might, eyes of flinted steel, any memory of the night past faded into nothingness.

The king's men with her crossed over to his side and she was surprised to see the deference they afforded him as she waited. He did not look in her direction once as he spoke of the plans for the ride towards Edinburgh.

He had insisted she wear her grey kirtle and blue bliaud from yesterday and the unfamiliarity of the long skirt against her legs annoyed her from the moment she had descended from her room.

She should have donned her hose and tunic, should have bound her plait tightly and laid a cap above it. Instead she had let the maid dress her hair, because Marc had asked it of her, and worn her unbecoming circular hat with the cloth tied beneath her chin.

Everything felt foreign. Even the hall of Ceann Gronna was different with the standards of the Dalceann clan removed and the furniture repositioned. She did not see one face she knew save for a young lad hovering around the door leading from the kitchens, worry in his expression, seeing her, no doubt, as a woman on the way to her death. Death after a night of full and unmitigated paradise. Even the thought made the muscles inside her clench in need, wanting it all to begin again in a rush of excitement.

Such craving brought blood to her cheeks, though catching the indifferent glance of Marc de Courtenay on her, she looked away.

She had made her bed and now must lie in it. The very thought unnerved her as he gestured her forwards.

'You shall ride in the cart with your maid, Lady Dalceann, and the soldiers of David will be set to guard you. We will make camp in the late afternoon and resume our journey tomorrow at first light, for the king is eager for your presence in Edinburgh.'

Not trusting speech, she merely nodded—*eager to behead me and use me as an example for what happens to a dissenter.*

She saw the truth in all of their eyes. If she had had her knife, she might have drawn it and ended it here, but Marc had taken it from her last night after he had left her bed, the warmth of his seed still within her, no precautions taken.

Used well and truly. She did not even recognise the woman she had become.

'Take her out.' Marc's command, no compassion in it.

She felt the arm of a soldier beneath her elbow shepherding her, and when his fingers touched the side of her breast he did not pull back.

A prisoner and a renegade. The rights of such women were diminished under the letter of the law. Lady Isobel Dalceann, the last of a clan that had no mind to follow ordinance and statute.

Lord above, if she looked anything other than what she did, all of this would have been so much easier,

Marc thought, restraining the urge to run a blade through the back of the man whose hands touched places that overstepped all boundaries.

With her pouting lips, dark eyes and hair, Isobel Dalceann seemed like a princess brought in from Anjou, the lines of her face so very fine and angled. He wished she had been plainer and not so generously curved and that the sensuality evident in her gold-tinged eyes was not unequivocally lascivious.

'It was never stated in any of the songs that Isobel Dalceann was such a great beauty.' Glencoe beside him said the words he could see all the others thinking.

'Save for the scar,' Mariner on his left added, 'though perhaps it only adds to her mystery. She will walk into the court of Edinburgh like a queen and the king will be mesmerised, just mark my words, for have you ever seen another like her?'

All who had heard the exchange shook their heads and a sense of unease began to turn inside Marc. He had thought it only him to be astounded by her, but here even seasoned married soldiers were admitting her charm.

Another thought blossomed. Perhaps in the world of the court, where comeliness was admired above all else, she might be saved.

An edge of guilt worried him, however. Had he ruined her chances by taking her to his bed? Would the king see the truth of what lay between them on

Isobel Dalceann's face when he asked of their relationship?

More lies.

He cursed. He had never been careless before. He had never pined for a woman the morning after, either, and there were still three whole days and nights before reaching Edinburgh.

If he had any honour at all, he would leave her alone and guide the hand of the king into setting up a union for her that would be both advantageous and effective. The very thought had him turning for the doorway and barking out orders to his men, irritation and rankle sending him outside to watch her step into a cart specially prepared to transport a prisoner.

As if she had known him to be there, she turned and stood still, a woman caught in the vagaries of war and holding her head up high. Her hands worried the fabric of her skirt, which had the effect of outlining the curve of her bottom, and he felt such a forcible hitch of want he wondered if she could see it even from such a distance. The path they had travelled together focused into this very second, a hundred people around observing them and a king who would need to be cajoled to be kind.

He could not jeopardise any of it by his own selfish want. She would find out exactly who he was when they reached Edinburgh. The faces of all the men he had slain came through the ether just as they did on nights when sleep seemed far away. A soldier who had hewn in blood and flesh a passageway for his life and far away from the charity of others.

A bastard child.

Even his name was not his own, but was one bestowed upon him as a squire by the lord he had trained under in Brittany. Girded with the sword, he had risen as another.

The only way he could save Isobel Dalceann here was by letting her go. His fingers caught the cold hilt of his dirk and he cursed roundly in the language of his long-dead mother.

Night covered the land and for once it seemed that the skies would stay clear and the fires lit as far as the eye could see would not be doused by the opening heavens. The tent Isobel shared with her maid was ample and well appointed, a pile of furs laid out for slumber and the leather the shelter was fashioned of thick and waterproof.

Only one day away from the town now. Tomorrow she would stand before the king and know her fate. Marc de Courtenay had not come near her since Ceann Gronna; even though she had searched for him amongst the columns of soldiers, he had been nowhere in sight.

She wanted to ask for him, to see whether he might come and reassure her with his presence. But he did not come and she did not ask.

Walking away from the tent towards a fire tended

by a single soldier, she breathed in the air with relief. The tent was stuffy and a headache had begun to form. She might be dead by this time tomorrow, her head adorning a stake on the castle walls, a warning to others who might think to disobey a king.

The glint of a sword in moonlight alerted her to the presence of another standing before a long line of bushes, lost in the shadow. She knew who it was by the fierce pull in her body and the unexpected rush of heat that left her breathless even before he spoke.

'I need to talk to you, Lady Dalceann.'

Stepping forwards, fire-flame caught Marc de Courtenay's face and she saw his clothes were very different from the ones he had favoured at the keep. He now wore a tunic in blue and gold, a black wolf embroidered on it, teeth bared and tongue lolling. A flicker of recognition came and went as she looked upon it, wondering where she might have seen such a badge. Danger and menace draped him now, the falchion and roundel dagger part of his personality in a way that they had not seemed to be before. The formality of his address worried her, too, the tone he used distant and impersonal, and she simply nodded because she could not trust herself to speak.

'We will come into Edinburgh around noon and the king will almost certainly summon you to court. David will ask for your fealty and your loyalty. He will demand your complete servitude. It is my advice that you give him these things irrespective of any allegiances you might already feel.'

She knew what he meant immediately. 'Allegiances such as the one held between us?' His glance met hers, the planes of his cheeks caught in the light, all hollows and angles.

'Yes.' The word was ground out hard and his reply pierced everything soft inside her. 'I can protect you only so far. You will need to do the rest yourself.'

'How?' The conversation had completely run away with her. 'How am I supposed to do that?' It felt as if they had never lain together in the high room on a bed of pelts.

'You are beautiful, Isobel. The most beautiful woman who will ever grace Edinburgh and David is a man of enough intelligence to understand the bargaining power of such comeliness.'

He sounded tired, the edge of defeat in his words surprising. The message he conveyed also concerned her.

'He would use me as a whore to trade favours with those who might pay?'

'Nae.' Snatching her hand into his own, he held it tight against his chest. She could feel the tension in him reverberate into her bones. 'Not as a whore, damn it, but as a wife.'

'Your wife?'

He let her go as if she had burnt him and moved back.

'There are things I have not told you, Isobel. Things that I should have maybe said...'

'You are married?'

'Not that.' The sound was soft against the winds of night. 'But I am a soldier whose existence is as precarious as your own, a soldier who survives under the shifting will of kings and in a hefty turn of coin.'

Isobel could not for a second understand exactly what it was he said. 'Who pays you?'

'Philip of France.' No warmth lingered as the truth fell bald between them. 'I am here to make certain that the Auld Alliance between Scotland and France is adhered to in the way my liege would want it to be.'

'Yet you came to Ceann Gronna as David's commander?'

'Every political promise demands much in the way of innocent blood. It is a fact.' He did not even flinch as he said it, his face a mask of indifference.

'Why are you telling me this now?'

'Because in another day everyone else will be and I wanted you to hear it first from me.'

'You would champion a cause even if you thought it unjust?'

'There are always two sides to every squabble, Lady Dalceann.'

'And you just choose the most lucrative? Like Ceann Gronna.'

When he did not answer she posed her own question.

'Work for me, then. Let me pay you in gold to order your men from their guard duty in the dungeons.' She could not bargain for herself, as she knew with the king's soldiers accompanying them it was far too late for that, but her clan might still be saved.

He shook his head. 'I cannot.' The soft certainty of his answer made it all the more final.

'Our night together meant nothing, then? Am I now only a woman whom you will sell for the greatest sum?'

'Nay, Isobel you are a woman I will protect by doing such.'

She drew back her hand and slapped his face so hard that her palm hurt. He didn't move an inch and the outline of redness showed above the deep tan of his skin.

'You are a coward to hide behind such untruth, Marc de Courtenay, and I would be a fool to take any such protection from you.' Everything between them shattered into pieces, all the honour she had imbued into their stolen nights, gone.

For a moment she thought he might say something to explain his actions, but he continued speaking as if nothing had happened, a mask across any emotion.

'Your gold will be placed into the hands of David as a surety. If you have knowledge of more, it might be wise to whet his appetite whilst pretending vagueness at the whereabouts. Anything of worth is a way of buying time. Remember that.'

'So this is the end of us, of our time together?'

'Nay, not quite.' Reaching forwards he brought his lips down across her own, the anger in him pulsing as his tongue sought that which she tried to deny. She felt his hands at her nape, holding her to his kiss, and his teeth scraped across her bottom lip as he let her go.

'Stay in the tent, Isobel. It is not safe for you to be out here alone.'

And then he was gone, the quiet sound of his footsteps the only thing that was left.

Her shaking fingers crept to her throat, feeling her pulse beneath, the beat racing against the promise of all that he had not offered, and she could not quite reconcile the man who had saved her at Ceann Gronna and kissed like that, with the soldier that he purported to be.

Marc leant back against the trunk of an elm, the rough ache of bark digging into his back like a penance.

God, but she got to him with her bravery and her beauty. The stalk of greenery he swiped at dropped to the earth and he ground the leaves beneath his feet till there was nothing left.

Like him!

He should not have kissed her, he knew he should not have, but the sadness in her eyes had been too much to bear and so he had.

For the first time ever he felt scared, for if anyone hurt her…

No. He would not think like that. He had to find a

way to keep Isobel Dalceann safe, no matter what it took. He saw her re-enter the tent and stayed watching for a good few hours past the midnight.

Mariner found him around three.

'I thought you would be somewhere here.'

He cocked his head, listening as the other spoke.

'The woman has a way of getting under your skin. It's her solitariness and her courage, I think, even aside from the way that she looks. Her father must have been a bastard. The men are taking bets on how long she will take to get the king beneath her spell.'

'I hope the odds are short.'

'Very. They have all fallen in love with her a little, I think.'

'She's barely spoken with them.'

'The Dalceann myth is strong, though, aye, and she does nothing to lessen it. Everyone talks of her skills with the sword and the way she filled out her lad's hose. Two sieges rebuffed and a campaign mounted in Ceann Gronna this time that was, at the least, salutary. Edinburgh will take to her like a man just out of the desert takes to water.'

Like me, Marc thought, balling his fists against his thighs. The place around his heart was tight and sore.

'Glencoe believes the king will marry her off to some rich baron who will never be able to control her. He says it would be a shame to see Lady Isobel Dalceann caged in by misunderstanding.'

Marc stood at that, the image of her in the arms of a man who would never care for her as much as he...

He stopped and put the thought away. Not for him. Not for him. Just keep her safe—that was all he could hope for—and then leave. The blackness in the heavens was endless when he looked up, the star of Sirius the brightest light in the sky.

He would remember her on this star in all the years of his life to come, he promised himself, from Burgundy or from the battlefields somewhere in the dangerous parts of the Kingdom of France and he would pray to God every evening for her happiness and satisfaction.

'I'll stand watch till the dawn.' Mariner's voice broke into his reveries and, knowing he needed some hours of rest to face the morrow, he left his lonely vigil and made for bed.

Chapter Fourteen

She kept her head up and her hands still as she waited in the company of Marc de Courtenay for an audience with the king.

A hundred people from the court of Edinburgh looked on, all their eyes pinned to her person. She did not glance directly at them, but above the height of their heads, so that she would not see what she supposed would be there.

Hatred and abhorrence.

She had heard the howls of anger directed towards her as they had made their way on foot up the Edinburgh Hill to the fortifications looming over them, tall houses crammed on each side and a smell unlike any she had ever encountered in the air.

Now here at the Great Castle Isobel could not remember another time when she had felt so afraid.

Marc beside her stood very still. War and battle walked with him like a companion, the greenness of his eyes exactly the colour she imagined menace might be, and watching everything.

Small flashes of him loving her came to mind, but it was as if a different man now remained in the place of the other. No one here could doubt his strength or his ability to deal with danger. She saw the same thought in the eyes of onlookers when she finally did deign to look.

So she was not the only one who had come to Edinburgh as an outlander. She wondered if he could feel the apprehension of the people as easily as she could, though the expression on his face suggested he had no mind for any of it. A loner. Philip's minion. A man whose very job defined him. Not one inch of his body looked anything other than in control.

A messenger finally approached and bade them forwards and double doors at one end of the room were opened.

Inside, at the head of a room filled with more people, Isobel could make out the throne of the king.

David the Second, King of the Scots, was not a large man or a particularly handsome one, but his eyes held the power of command and right now they were laid upon her person.

'Lady Isobel Dalceann, my lord,' a voice rang out. 'The Chief of the Dalceann clan at Ceann Gronna keep in Fife and Sir Marc de Courtenay, the Wolf of Burgundy.'

The Wolf of Burgundy?

Isobel had heard that name so very many times in the years of her growing up. The Wolf of Burgundy was Marc de Courtenay, a warlord whose campaigns across the wider world had been the stuff of the songs of bards and minstrels for a decade?

A man of bloodshed and battle. Had he not tried to tell her that last night? This was the man who seldom took prisoners and one who collected coin for all the souls who came against him. Even her name was as nothing compared to his own!

Her world focused as the breath she held was punched from her body. She did not dare to look at him as David the King of the Scots continued to speak.

'Home from the wild coast of Fife and a profitable campaign by the look, too. Do you have anything to say about it, de Courtenay?'

'Indeed, sire.' Marc bowed, the movement rough and awkward, lifting his head as he began to speak, his voice unhurried and steady.

'Ceann Gronna is a keep that is now in the hands of the Scottish Crown, the last of its soldiers guarded in the dungeons. Glencoe and I crossed from the north this morning. The Earl of Huntworth, Archibald McQuarry, died by the sword after he broke all the rules of treaty and tried to steal gold marked as your bounty, my lord.'

'And where is this gold now?'

'It is here and at your disposal.'

Isobel saw him place a sackcloth bag, specially furnished with handles and double bound in leather, at the king's feet. She knew the load would be heavy, though it seemed in the way he held it to be as light as a feather. Grinding her teeth together, she did her best to appear a maid with little in the way of choice.

'Was the keep razed?'

'Nae. It lies intact, my lord.'

'A treasure to be added to my stock, then, de Courtenay. Well done.'

'The Chief of the clan of Dalceann, Lady Isobel, comes to the castle, too, sire. She comes under the weight of her father's poor judgement, for it was Donald Dalceann who started the canker that has destroyed Ceann Gronna, giving his daughter no alternative but to try to save its people.'

'Step forwards.' David's voice brooked no disobedience as he gestured to her and Isobel tried her very hardest to appear as Marc had just stated it, the beleaguered offspring of an unwise parent.

'You do not look like a witch,' he said at length. 'You do not have the appearance of one who has sold their soul to the Devil at all. What say you, de Courtenay?'

'I say she is a woman who has been misled by the men around her. I say that the stories of her here in Edinburgh are false and that she bears the mark of her father's duplicity on her cheek and nothing more.

'I also say that around her neck I found this.' He

pulled out a chain and held it up. On the end of the silver was a tooth yellowed from age and inlaid on an ornate clasp. 'When I took it from her she did not disappear into a puff of smoke as some said she would, sire. The trinket was nothing more than the denture of some marine animal found on the beaches around Ceann Gronna and kept as a reminder of the power of that which lies close by in the sea. No more than that. Lady Isobel Dalceann comes before you today, sire, with sorrow in her heart for the trouble her keep has caused you and the hope that the promise of more gold might be enough to let you understand her contrition and allow her to state abject loyalty to your cause.'

'You words are strong, Sir Marc.' The king stood and walked forwards so that he stood beside her, almost a half a head shorter than she was. She tried to curtsy in a way that was appropriate and did not look at him, as she had been instructed.

When he lifted her chin, though, she had no other course but to meet his eyes. Fear held her immobile.

'She is an admirable beauty. A rare and untarnished treasure. It would be a shame to see such comeliness gone.'

Isobel swallowed. Did he mean that it would be?

Marc, however, was not quite finished.

'When you sent me into the lands of Fife, you made the promise of a reward should I come back with a triumph. My one wish is that Lady Isobel Dalceann be allowed to show her loyalty to the cause of Scotland and to your kingship, sire.'

David stood still, watching Marc closely and running his fingers over the beard that covered his chin. Finally he spoke to her.

'Sir Marc goes a long way to hold up the surety of your disposition, Lady Dalceann. Is this what you would also will?'

'I would, sire.' She hated the way her voice shook.

'Do you swear your allegiance to me here and now in this court?'

'I do, my liege.'

'Very well. You shall abide here in the House of Bruce for the next month. If you appear genuine and biddable, I shall marry you to one of my barons. And if not…'

He left the other option unspoken.

'De Courtenay, I shall for ever be in the debt of your patron Philip the Sixth of France for sending you to me. I will hold a feast in the castle tomorrow in honour of the victory. I shall expect you to attend.'

A flick of his fingers and they were shepherded out another door to their left, a new group of people coming before the king.

Isobel felt Marc at her side and the fall of his embroidered bliaud touched hers, though when he stopped to let her move in front of him the moment was lost.

At the next door a servant of the king gestured her to follow him.

'Will it be safe?' she asked of Marc in her quietest voice, their argument from yesterday lost beneath the weight of an unfamiliar court.

'For now,' he answered. 'But do not let your guard down.'

Then he was gone and she was alone, walking through the corridors of a castle in the company of her servant and two court maids who had fallen in behind her, both dressed in garments so very much more elaborate than her own.

Marc strode back through the anterooms with purpose. He had seen the way she looked at him when his name had been called.

The Wolf of Burgundy.

Usually the epithet was useful in his maintenance of distance from others, the legend of stories about him affording a fright that held questions at bay.

With Isobel he had only seen the anger.

He had also seen the look of surprise on her face when he had drawn out the tooth on her chain—the yellowed whale's ivory, with its ornate silver casing, exactly right. But lies required careful management and it was his experience that using part of a lie always made the facts so much more believable. People wanted the myth explained, and the best way to do that was with the showmanship of half-truths.

Half-truths to save her life, but have her married

off to one of David's barons? Caution beat hard as he tried to reconcile her safety with such an outcome and failed.

His head ached with the complexity of it all. He had little sway here apart from a reputation in battle and an unacknowledged family connection with Philip of France.

It was not enough to stand forth himself and ask for Isobel's hand in marriage. He was a bastard and he was half-French. He had never been part of the fabric of the society of Scotland and Isobel would need that if she were to survive here.

He hoped like hell that David would adhere to the protection promised and that the House of Bruce did not hold an assassin who might profit from the death of a known dissenter, even given the king's leniency.

Madeline.

His wife's name came unbidden, a good decade of years after her murder. He had thought her safe, too. The wind in the corridors of the castle whistled cold against stone, just as they had in Burgundy when he had found her lifeless body swollen with a child who would never be born.

Madeline. Soft and pliant. Trusting and open. Such goodness had killed her in the end.

The hard core of Isobel Dalceann was part of the reason he was attracted to the Chief of the Dalceann. She would not be duped by treachery and she could fight better than many a man.

He smiled. With her at his side he could probably rule the world.

A group of men walking the other way stopped to let him pass. Marc recognised the face of Stuart McQuarry, the new Earl of Huntworth, the sly look in his eyes exactly the same as his brother's.

With ten others around him in a public place McQuarry stepped forwards. 'You may think to trick David into sheltering Lady Dalceann, de Courtenay, but two of my family lie dead at the keep of Ceann Gronna with no justice for either of them. Believe me, someone is going to pay.'

'Isobel Dalceann is under David's protection. Be careful how you tread with such accusations, or there may not be any Huntworth brothers left.'

'Is that a threat?'

Marc shook his head. 'Nay, it is a fact. The king does not take too kindly to those who would advocate harm to his guest.'

'The Dalceann woman is here to dupe him. Likely she will run her knife through someone before the week is gone, given her reputation.'

'Then let her discredit herself. No point in your sacrifice for a cause which is lost anyway.'

The mood changed around him. Subtly. Had he bought Isobel time or just lost her some? She would need to be warned, of course, and the group standing before him would require watching. He catalogued their faces for his future reference. The court in Scotland held as much intrigue as the French one and he had always been adept at navigating menace. McQuarry, however, was not finished.

'Others might be scared of you, de Courtenay, but I am not one of them and an interloper sent here by the French king can only be tolerated for so long.'

'I agree.' Smiling, he stepped back to let them past, these men of poor judgement and poorer diplomacy, but by experience he knew that those who felt marginalised were always dangerous. His mind returned to the arrow which had almost killed him at the Ceann Gronna keep. Was treachery a trait born into the sons of McQuarry?

His left hand gripped the dagger at his belt as he watched them go.

Chapter Fifteen

Margaret, her maid, primped her hair until it fell in a full plait down her back, the sides drawn into fine strands and fastened with a brooch of gold.

Everything on her person was borrowed for the afternoon's feast. The gown of red brocade, the belt of ornately beaded dark-blue silk and a surcoat to match. They had been left in her chamber without explanation and Isobel knew the king would expect her to wear such luxury.

The options closed in as she looked at herself. She knew she needed to confuse the court here in order to survive, and tonight she was to play the downcast beauty brought in to show off her family's regret at disobeying a monarch.

The woman looking back at her was hardly recognisable. Even the scar on her cheek had been disguised by a potion mixed from clay and the hat with a long and floating veil gave added height to her tallness.

Only the eyes were hers, steeped in watchfulness and vigilance. She softened her glance, adding in a touch of confusion just for good measure.

Would Marc de Courtenay be there today? Would she be able to converse with him? Would he take one look at her and know the pretence, the only person in the world who might understand such protections?

Her Wolf of Burgundy?

The thought made her smile, for to tame such a one would be to destroy him. She knew it without thinking, for the wild menace was so much a part of what drew her to him.

Lady Helen Cunningham had been assigned to her as companion, and the woman was most generous with her praise.

'You will take the fancy of each and every man at court who has the need of a wife, my dear,' she said softly, her eyes a dewy blue. 'Why, if they do not instantly fall to their knees and declare their feelings, I should be most surprised'.

Isobel smiled, because it seemed to be expected and because such a thing was exactly what she would not favour.

'No, no.' The woman hurried forwards. 'Show no emotion that will pucker the handiwork my maid has applied to your cheek. The clay is oiled, but will crack under any such pressure.'

Such a directive suited her and she nodded her acquiescence, the necessity of a forced jubilation gone.

She wondered if eating might not have the same effect, but did not mention it. She was starving and the smells of the palace kitchens had wafted up to her rooms all morning.

'Everyone will be here, of course. All the most handsome men from Scotland. From what I hear, Sir Marc de Courtenay is the one all the women would prefer, but his lack of land and family name preclude him from being one of King David's candidates. His reputation also marks him as ungovernable, of course, though there are rumours his father could well be from these climes.'

Isobel's interest flared at the new subject of conversation and she was disappointed when the woman switched topics.

'But enough of fancy. The McFadden brothers are more than eligible and the last McQuarry son is on the lookout for a bride. A strangely morose boy, I always thought, but the family lands are extensive and fertile.'

McQuarry. Her skin crawled even with the thought of the name as she followed the woman along the corridor to the Great Hall. Lady Helen was a gossip, but her love of talking might prove useful in making sense of this court.

She didn't seem to harbour any animosity towards the Dalceann intransigence, either, which was a decided boon.

As the chatter of a large group of people came

closer, Isobel felt nervous in a way she seldom did. It was the unfamiliarity of the setting, she supposed, and wished again that Marc de Courtenay might have been at her side.

Isobel Dalceann came into the room like a queen, head held high and in a gown of crimson designed to show off the darkness of her hair and eyes, and her curves.

The room quietened as the topic of all conversation took her seat at the table of the king. Her back was straight and her face expressionless and from this distance Marc could make out no sign of the scar. A pity that, he thought sagely, for the make-up hid a feature that defined her. Different. Brave. Original.

He sat at the very end of the same table by the door. It was a habit of his, born from a lifetime of danger, and he did not move into Isobel's sight as he saw her glance around. No jeopardy here yet, he thought, the dagger in his belt easily accessible should any peril materialise.

David called for quiet and motioned for Isobel Dalceann to stand. She looked like a woman who was more than grateful to her liege for the unexpected opportunity of proving her worth in a court that was inclined to fear her, and her beauty shone out like a beacon. Marc applauded such a tactic, her feminine docility used as a weapon with points as sharp as any sword.

'Lady Isobel Dalceann comes to Edinburgh as my guest, a woman wronged by the stories which have circulated about her.' The king's voice brooked no argument and Marc watched as Isobel bowed her head, her previous defiance now turned into shame. If he didn't know her better, even he would have believed such temperance. The next words took humour away.

'In the coming weeks it is my wish she be betrothed to one of my lords at court, so that the Ceann Gronna keep in Fife can be returned to the defence of Scotland under my tutelage.'

Around him the talk mounted, the younger knights at a table to his left saying what all the unmarried men in the room felt.

'If I could get her into bed, I would never stray.'

'If you could get her into bed, you would need a good deal more money than you have and a keep that was at least as large as Ceann Gronna.'

'Do you think David is in love with her himself?'

'Who wouldn't be? She has the face of an angel.'

'And the body of a siren.'

'Enough of all the conjecture, lads.' An older man who Marc had not seen before sat down. 'King David will choose her husband, mark my words, and it won't be the likes of us.'

Or of him! That truth had Marc lifting a tankard from a passing servant and downing it in one unbroken swallow.

But the king was not finished. 'Pray tell us, Lady Dalceann, just what attributes you would find attractive in a husband?'

Dark eyes scanned the room, and as she shifted her position and turned slightly her glance came into direct contact with his. Had she known he was there all along? Marc was inclined to believe that she might have.

'Honesty and loyalty, my liege,' she replied, the message between them so powerful he felt the shock of it burn through his body. All the things that he had not given her. He looked away and the room closed in with laughter and noise as Stuart McQuarry raised his glass.

'To Lady Dalceann,' he called out. 'May she choose well.'

'You are implying interest, then, my lord?' David waited for his answer.

'Indeed, I am, my liege.'

Other voices called out their claims, too, and the anger that had threatened inside Marc all night boiled over. Leaving his pewter mug on the table, he walked outside, striding along the corridors until he found himself in the courtyard proper, Edinburgh sprawled before him in the afternoon light.

Placing his hands palm down on warm stone, he felt a sense of impotence he had never known before, as he remembered the feel of Isobel Dalceann against him curled into safety.

* * *

She saw him go, a man apart from all the others, his largeness here marking him out as a knight of wars and battle. He had not called his name, though every fibre of her being wished that he might have shouted it out and that David would countenance such a proposal.

The need for caution and a dutiful appearance tugged at her, too; her dress was tight in the places that she knew were provocative, a deliberate ploy by the king to net the richest baron and the most in the way of tithes. She was suddenly sick of it, this game of politics and coin, as the only man who could have held Ceann Gronna safe for ever disappeared into the sunny afternoon.

'You have created a flurry, Lady Dalceann.' The Earl of Carr on the other side of her leaned over. 'And a new problem—how is our king to pick one ardent suitor above others and still manage to keep the peace?'

'I should prefer no suitors whatsoever, my lord,' she returned and saw the man's face pucker up into humour. Helen Cunningham was speaking to a woman on the other side of the table, allowing Isobel a moment of unobserved honesty.

'Because your father and husband led you so far astray? Indeed, I can well see your point.'

Alisdair's face came before her in memory, a man of logic, reason and good sense. To hear his name

slandered here in the court of the king to help her
cause was neither fair nor right, and she ground her
teeth together, an action that had the effect of dis-
lodging the heavy make-up now dried upon her skin.
Small pieces of it fell on to the tablecloth, the mask
of Lady Cunningham's maid being replaced by truth.
Wiping off the rest, she did not look away from the
face of the Earl beside her. Rather, she enjoyed the
consternation of those in close proximity and as
she smiled she knew the puckered skin would be at
its most noticeable.

This was who she was: the last chieftain of Ceann
Gronna now placed upon a bidding block to be sold
for the highest offer. Let them know what it was they
tendered for, these minions of David with little else
to speak of save the beauty they craved. The slice
of her father's blade had only been a part of it; the
words he had shouted as he had tried to murder her
far more lasting.

'I curse your mother for taking the only son I ever
had to his death at sea and I curse you for looking
exactly like her.' Ian had had him around the neck by
that stage and so she was spared from hearing more.

The cut across her cheek, however, had made her
much less like the woman he hated and much more
like the man he was. Angry. Intemperate and un-
trusting.

The people here had been nurtured and cared for,
much the same as the plants that Alisdair had grown

in the heated houses in the bailey of the keep when the weather grew colder. She could not blame them for the looks they gave her now, their more normal politeness askew with alarm and growing apprehension.

When the meal was finished and the king had taken his leave, Isobel placed the knife she held carefully down in front of her and moved towards the windows on the other side of the room.

'If you stay in the vicinity of another woman at an occasion like this, it makes it much easier to beg an excuse from the unwanted advances of men.'

Isobel looked around at the older woman who spoke to her. She was tall and thin, blonde curls falling down her back into a heavy net of gold.

'I beg your pardon?'

'It does not pay to stand alone here, Lady Dalceann, especially in your position.'

'My position?'

'The position of a woman who is not in love with any of the suitors the king offers. It makes you fair game.'

Isobel pushed down the urge to smile. Few people here in court were so honest.

'But forgive me, I am Lady Catriona, the daughter of the Earl of Roseheath, one of King David's strongest supporters.'

'Then you probably should not be seen speaking with me.'

The woman ignored her altogether. 'Fathers have much to answer for. Take my own case, for example. My father married me off to a man who was twenty years my senior and wondered why I then took on a series of lovers to balance the redress. You, of course, could do exactly the same given David's edicts, for it should be said that politics makes whores of any thinking woman.'

Again Isobel tried not to smile, the relief of a female who was neither tongue tied in her presence nor full of censure, enormous. Was Lady Catriona always this forthright?

'I am not certain that the ability to argue against the plans of men is something to be lauded here.' Isobel tried to keep her voice down as the other shook her head.

'They leave me alone because I was the wife of one powerful man and I am the daughter of another. They leave you alone because no one here is certain of you. I can see it in their faces. The court holds its breath to see what it is you might do next.'

'I am a prisoner, my lady. There is little that I can control.'

Lord, she had no notion of the true connections of this woman and Marc had instructed her to take care and trust no one.

'Myth helps you, of course. The Underworld holds its own superstitions.'

'Pardon?'

'The tooth de Courtenay pulled from your neck. You were supposed to disappear in a puff of smoke after such a happening. It was clever of him to use the magic.'

At that moment Marc walked back into the great chamber, his height allowing him to be spotted easily.

'Now there is one who would make sure a woman would never wander, Lady Dalceann. A man whom you watch when nobody thinks you are looking. Sir Marc is perhaps not all he is thought to be, however. It is said his father was a Scottish lord who travelled to the court of Burgundy and sired a child with a relative of the French King. On the grounds of that information, his father could have even been my husband.'

Something in the tone of the older woman's voice made Isobel wary. 'Who was…?'

'Cameron McQuarry. The old Earl of Huntworth. I was made his second wife when the mother of his sons passed away.'

Light green eyes held hers, unwavering and forthright. Was this advice given in warning or in guidance?

'I could, of course, confront de Courtenay personally with such information, but I think it far more judicious if it came from you.'

'From me? I barely know him.' Her heart began to beat faster beneath the gown of red silk.

'Oh, come, Lady Dalceann. All tales tell me that you are far more honest than that. Besides, the warlord was in your bed at Ceann Gronna and rumour has it there were no cries of discontent.'

'You have asked after me?' Danger in the royal court was many faceted and even the aristocratic face of a high-born lady was not to be discounted.

'Nay, it is de Courtenay that I am intrigued by,' she answered.

Was it entrapment this woman offered—the chance to ensnare a commander of men and ruin him should such petition prove to be unwarranted?

'The politics of diplomacy hold no shelter for a man of war who might wrongly claim a family name that was never his.' Another thought then occurred to her. 'Does Stuart McQuarry suspect the same?'

'He is clever, Lady Dalceann, so I imagine the idea must have occurred to him. Especially as de Courtenay has the look of the old Earl.'

'And did the old Earl acknowledge de Courtenay as his offspring?'

Catriona McQuarry frowned. 'There is no one answer, Lady Dalceann, but a hundred other half-truths. Give de Courtenay this crest. Ask if he recognises it.' Lady Catriona twisted a ring from her finger and handed it over beneath the cover of a long train looped across her arms.

'Know also that de Courtenay watches every move you make, and carefully.' Her green eyes were measured. 'If by any chance the ring should go astray and fall into the hands of those who may misuse it, I will deny the fact that I ever gave it to you, just as I will disavow the topic of this particular conversation.'

With that she moved away into the company of a group of men, who welcomed her warmly. Lovers, perhaps, given what she had said, or merely acquaintances?

The information she had just imparted made Isobel jumpy for fear others might see what she now imagined. Marc could have killed his own brother when he had run Archibald McQuarry through with his swordplay at Ceann Gronna. She looked over at the group he stood amongst, but he did not look her way once.

Stuart McQuarry was not so reticent. He approached her almost as soon as Lady Catriona had left her side, a sneer on his face, and she felt the same edgy loathing that she had for his brother.

'Lady Dalceann.' His eyes ran across the tight bliaud at her breast and lingered there for longer than was appropriate. 'I think it is only fair that you should know the other ladies in court spurn Lady Catriona as a gossip full of impossible falsehoods.'

Isobel felt the ring in her palm and remained silent.

'With only a few weeks until the king wants you

betrothed, I thought it timely to speak to you about my own situation. I am the last of the McQuarrys.'

Perhaps not quite the last. The voice inside her was strong.

'My castle stands on the hills above Stirling on a property five times the size of your own and my family holds close to the ear of the king.'

He had shifted now, his leg almost up against her own. 'As one of your suitors I would enjoy the chance to get to know you better.'

His breath smelt of rancid deceit, if an emotion could be given a scent, and even in court, not ten yards from Marc de Courtenay, she felt scared, the vestiges of Stuart McQuarry's late brother's pawing making her stomach turn. Catching the floaty material cascading from her hat, she held it tight so that he should not try to take her hand.

For the first time she saw Marc glance her way.

'King David has given me leave to take you riding towards the west of Edinburgh town. Perhaps we might make the journey tomorrow.'

She shook her head, trying to appear puzzled.

'Nay. There is some other important thing that I am to do, but I cannot for the life of me remember what it is.' Scattiness in a woman was always a protection because men expected it and made allowances.

'Then the following day…'

Again she shook her head. 'A friend has asked me

to accompany her on an outing to see her mother. I could not disappoint her.'

As if on cue Catriona McQuarry came again to her side. 'I am sorry, Lady Isobel. I meant to return sooner, but I was waylaid. Huntworth.' She held out her hand and snatched it back the moment that she could, the frosty reception seeming to convince Stuart McQuarry of the wisdom of withdrawal.

When he left Catriona smiled. 'He is a man to be avoided at all costs.'

'I know.'

'Good. Then let us sit and pretend that we have all the topics in the world to converse about. That should keep him and the others well away from us.'

Marc watched Huntworth leave the room, as he circled around Isobel and Catriona McQuarry to stand with Dougal MacDonald, an older man he had known well in Burgundy a good ten years earlier.

He had seen the woman pass something over to Isobel hidden under the folds of a veiled train. The intrigue of it made him uneasy.

'Lady Isobel Dalceann is comely,' MacDonald said as he saw where he looked. 'I hear there are a good many names in the pile for her hand in marriage. Huntworth's is the one most are favouring.'

'Is yours there?' Marc swallowed his drink as he asked the question.

'Nae, I am too old for such a game, but if Stuart

McQuarry is allowed to win the hand of Lady Isobel, I fear for her well-being, for he is every bit like his father.'

The warning was quietly given and Marc nodded. 'From my limited knowledge of them I think the whole family is cankered through and through.'

'Torwood, the family castle at Stirling, is formidable. Few barons could claim such a stronghold.'

Torwood. His mother had written the same unusual name in the front of her Bible that had been passed down to him. Marc had always wondered why it should be there, though his aunt had never been forthcoming. Indeed, when he had shown her the scrawl on a trip back to the courts of Burgundy when he was training as a squire, she had torn the page from the book and hurled the crumpled sheet into the fire.

'Your mother was a woman easily duped by a handsome face. Take care that you are not as trusting.'

By then he had long lost any belief in the goodness of others; his training under Philip's patronage was harsh and cruel. He did not show her a letter that he had found tucked into the back end of the same Bible with the name written again under a crest of three blue stars on a white background.

'Is the old McQuarry still alive?'

MacDonald looked at him strangely. 'Nay. He lived by the sword and he died by it. A disgruntled squire finished him off, if I remember rightly. All of his sons seem sworn to the same code of violence.'

Marc was suddenly aware that Stuart McQuarry was sidling closer so he brought the conversation to an end.

He also saw that Isobel watched him closely from the other side of the room.

Torwood. He hoped the word did not link him into the ancestry of the McQuarrys with all of his heart.

A good two hours later Marc found himself outside the part of the castle that housed Lady Dalceann. Leaning up against a tree in the courtyard beneath the high towers of her room, he watched to see that nothing untoward was happening anywhere near her person, just as he had done all the way down to Edinburgh from Ceann Gronna.

She would not see him, he knew that, but it was nice to stand and listen to the sounds and know that she would be hearing them, too: the call of a night bird, a dog barking further down the hill, the last of the revellers leaving a tavern, strong drink making them rowdy and indiscreet.

He imagined the sounds at the keep as he stood there, the sea against the rocks endlessly turning. Swearing, he wondered why the castle drew him back as it did, for he had travelled all of his life, seldom glancing across his shoulder at what had been left behind.

Tonight he felt homeless and stateless, the stigma of his birth magnified here by all those with long and venerable family histories.

His blood line could be traced to this city, too, he mused, the unexpected mention of the Torwood name burning as curiosity and wonder beneath the more forceful denial.

The glint of steel near his temple had him reeling and he leapt away from the downward thrust of a sword, his fingers finding his dagger and hurling it outwards. The heavy clunk of a blade hit bone, followed by the soft drop of a body before three more men were on him.

McQuarry's men. He recognised their faces even as he made short work of their attack, the city lords' aggression no match at all for years and years of seasoned warfare.

He did not even bother to take their weapons from them as he reclaimed his knife, wiped it against the fine velvet of one of his assailants' surcoats and made his way back into the winding corridors of the castle.

Chapter Sixteen

Isobel could not sleep for the fear of all that had happened across the past few days.

Since his decree, twenty suitors had been presented to her at various times by a monarch who would like nothing better than to have her married off to one of them and to be settled again at Ceann Gronna, the problem of the keep solved neatly.

The faces of those who had offered for her hand swam in unison through the gloom of the night. Some were good men and kind men. Some like Huntworth made her skin crawl every time he reached out to touch her under this pretext or that.

None made her feel like Marc de Courtenay did and there was the trouble. She no longer wanted only a union that was political or pragmatic, even given Ceann Gronna and its people were the prize she might receive because of it. Nae, all she wanted was what she had enjoyed with Marc again, long hours filled with pleasure.

She moved her legs against the memory and her fingers crept to the space between her thighs, although a noise outside her window made her hold her breath and listen. The leaves of the tree against her wall rustled in the wind as they had done for all of the time she had been here and the sound of voices further away was not worrying, for the castle was busy far into the evening, silence coming only in the very small hours.

But someone was out there. She felt it in her bones.

Her hand found the blade she had taken from a soldier in the Great Hall who had no notion of her quick fingers at his belt. The weapon was comforting and she had sharpened its edges against stone, honed to gleaming.

Slipping out of bed, she went across to the glass, the expensive unfamiliar shininess so much easier to see out of than the oiled linens at Ceann Gronna. No shadow lurked where it should not have and she relaxed slightly, jolted a moment later when the lock on her door began to vibrate.

Someone was breaking in. To kill her? She did not scream or shout. She was perfectly capable of dealing with this herself, weapon in hand and surprise on her side.

The offender came in less than ten seconds later and she had the blade at his neck, ready to slice deep when some echo of familiarity stopped her.

'It's me.'

'Lord. I could have killed you.'

'Good.' Marc turned to look at her then, the line of red at his throat where she had pressed down making her realise how close she had come to a mistake.

'Why didn't you fight?'

'The door was not shut and I didn't want to alert the guards.'

His eyes ran across the dagger even as he pulled a cloth from beneath his heavy mantle and opened it.

'This is a second option,' he said quietly. 'I did not realise you already had a first.'

His knife was longer than the one she held, but every bit as sharp.

'Do not let McQuarry anywhere near you if you are by yourself.'

As the moonlight fell across his face she saw what he meant. With a black eye and a gouged cheek Marc de Courtenay looked the very picture of a wounded soldier.

'Four men waited for me this evening in the quieter parts of the castle grounds. I recognised them from Huntworth's group.'

'They let you go?'

'I made them.'

The hollow empty loneliness that had been her constant companion for so many days welled up and she turned away, not wanting him to see what she knew would be so very plain in her eyes. Replacing the knife under her pillow, she took a breath before facing him again.

'How did you get in here without being seen?'

'Every hall is full of shadows. I used them.'

'If they find you—'

He did not let her finish. 'They won't. I have had word that your men from the keep have been given reprieve on the promise that they stay in Fife and never raise arms again, save in the name of the king. I think David will leave them there until you return to Ceann Gronna.'

Relief made Isobel feel light-headed. It was all Marc's doing, of course. No one else in the world made her feel so emotional.

'David would like the castle fully functional by the autumn equinox, so your suitors are expecting a late summer wedding.'

'Nay, there is not one here that I would wish to marry.'

He brought his finger up against her bottom lip and the words died as he brushed it carefully.

'Shhh.'

The noise of people in the corridor passed them by, revellers from the day's celebration taking them into the small hours. When there was silence again he spoke as quietly as he could.

'Catriona McQuarry gave you something today in the hall?'

Isobel smiled. She should have known that Marc

would have seen the exchange, for even when he was not looking he noticed things.

Walking across to the bed, she extracted the ring from beneath her mattress. 'It was this. She bade me to tell you that your father could well be the old Earl of Huntworth. Do you recognise it?'

The crest of the ring caught the firelight.

'I was born in the last few breaths of my mother's life as the result of a brief affair with a man she should never have lain with. What makes Lady Catriona think it could be him?'

'She said that you have the look of him.'

Shaking his head, he handed her back the ring. 'If I fought my battles on such flimsy evidence, I would never have won a fight.'

She could tell he wanted to go. Already he was looking towards the door, his head tilted to the outside noises.

Disappointment blossomed.

'You will come again?'

He seemed distant and ill at ease.

'I will try.'

She wanted to reach out and touch his face, hurt by the fighting. She wanted to ask him to stay for the night until the early morning dawn and have him hold her just as he had done at Ceann Gronna.

But he was already opening the door and instructing her to lock it after him, as he slipped out amongst the long-fallen shadows.

* * *

The web around Isobel grew—first the threat of being an insurgent and now a new one, for the three blue stars against a plain background were etched like a tattoo into his memory.

The Earl of Huntworth? His mind turned with the possibility. Everything he had ever heard of Cameron McQuarry had been unflattering, a violent and ill-tempered man of little repute.

Lord help him, that this was the father he had come to find, and why had the McQuarry woman shown the ring to Isobel and not to him?

There had been a message, too, delivered to his door the first night of his return: *watch your back and ask no questions.*

No questions about his father or no questions about Isobel Dalceann? He had set Mariner to watch the steps leading to his room for any movement while he was not there and he had seen only a thin, tall boy pass by. Tall and thin, like Lady Catriona, delivering a warning that she would later emphasise in the giving of the ring?

Nothing made any sense any more.

Nothing except for the feeling that when Isobel Dalceann was close in his arms, her dark eyes edged in gold promised him everything.

The list of enemies grew around them and no indication of who exactly they were. Another thought made him stop in his tracks. Was his presence in

Isobel Dalceann's life bringing a danger that could kill her in the end?

Like Madeline. She had died at the hand of a man who hated him. Could the same happen here in Scotland?

Sharp pain lanced a part of his chest that had for so many years lain dormant.

It was time to find out exactly who the old Earl of Huntworth had been.

Isobel knelt at the gilded font of the small chapel in the castle and prayed. No one else seemed to use this tiny room. Candles burnt around her, their scent strong in the small space.

She was therefore surprised when a voice took her from her devotions.

'I thought you might be here.' Lady Catriona made her way in and sat at one of the two pews. 'Did you manage to show de Courtenay the ring?' Her question was softly voiced.

'I did, though he had not seen such a badge before.'

'He told you that?'

There was a tone in her words that worried Isobel. Digging into her surcoat, she handed the ring back, watching as the woman replaced it on her finger.

'Did your husband ever mention Marc to you?'

'No, not to me. He was not the sort who enjoyed the art of conversation, you understand. I was married to him for five years and every one of those days seemed like for ever. You have no idea of the horror of a marriage that demeans you, Lady Dalceann, for by all accounts here your husband was ineffective but kind. I was twenty-two when my father sent me to Stirling and almost thirty when he finally died. It is not revenge I now seek, but justice. A child of the Huntworths has been lost to the whims of history and the estate is wealthy. I look at Marc de Courtenay and I think he should have the chance to know his bloodlines.'

For the first time since meeting Catriona McQuarry, Isobel saw fear behind bravado.

'Why do you think he could be related if no proof exists?'

'I did not say that there was none. Sometimes when the old Earl didn't think others watched him he would drag out a box full of mementos. De Courtenay's name was on every single one of them.'

'Where is the box now?

'At the Huntworth estate of Torwood, I should imagine. I am not welcome there any more and Stuart McQuarry is hardly going to locate it for me.'

'But you think that Marc might be able to prove he is a McQuarry should he find it.'

The other woman nodded quite forcibly. 'I know you like him, Isobel, and as the lost child of such a family he might be able to stand up and be counted as a suitor. You remind me of myself many years ago, you see, and I think if only there had been someone around who could have helped me I would be a different person now. A happier one.'

She turned the ring on her finger, and it glinted in the candlelight. 'My stepson Stuart McQuarry is a dangerous adversary, however, and you will have to be careful in your search for answers.' She stopped, her voice tapering off for a second as she took breath. 'I cannot come alone and meet you again because if Huntworth should see me, then he may make certain I can no longer talk to anyone.'

'He would kill you?'

Her eyes filled with fire. 'When Marc de Courtenay ran his sword through Archibald McQuarry at the keep of Ceann Gronna, half of my problems were solved. It is another thing that I owe him for.'

'If I can be of any assistance—'

Catriona did not let her finish. 'You have already helped me, Lady Dalceann, because in you I see a woman who will not be subjected to the flagrant will of men. It is my sanctuary.'

There was another gathering in the castle the following afternoon and Marc de Courtenay sat at the top table in the seat next to hers.

Isobel could not mask her surprise as she was shown to her place, as he was dressed in clothes she had not seen him wear before, his rich russet-velvet tunic belted by a leather strap that was encrusted in jewels. The wolf motif was embroidered in the material at his neckline.

In the company of others Isobel felt less certain about their relationship, the intimacy of their nighttime trysts relegated here to formality and manners. There was no memory of any confidence or closeness as he raised his eyes to hers.

'I hope you are faring well in the castle, Lady Dalceann,' he said, to all intents and purposes a stranger asking after her well-being.

'Indeed, Sir Marc. I have been welcomed most warmly.' Further afield on the long benches people watched, the eyes of the court upon them. It was a role they played out here she understood, a woman who had been brought to the court by a commander of men. Only politics and war, no love in it.

Love.

She blushed at the very word because all she wanted to do was to lay her fingers across his hard brown hand and hold on for ever.

When he picked up his bread she saw that he wore a ring engraved with two lions and many fleur-de-lis. The Valois insignia. She had seen a drawing of it in a manuscript in the chapel at the keep. Why would he wear it, then, in the company of another king if the claims within it were false?

Another thought occurred. Perhaps they were not false. A further thought occurred on top of that one.

Yesterday he had said he did not recognise the badge of the Huntworths, but could that have been a lie, too?

She longed to tell him of her suspicions and Catriona McQuarry's confession, but here and now was neither the time nor the place. Here they were David's guests in a castle where one wrong word could have consequences.

'Your exploits in France are legendary, Sir Marc. Have you taken place in the tournaments of Burgundy at all?'

Such a vapid question but all she could think of with the man next to her listening in on their conversation.

'Once or twice I have, though a good many years ago now.'

The blonde-haired Anne of Kinburn further down the table laughed in the way women here often did, all artifice and no humour.

'You could take my favour with you into any arena any time you want, Sir Marc.' The tone in her voice was honey sweet. 'How long will you be staying here in Edinburgh?'

Alabaster-smooth skin and the full promise of cleavage were easily seen in the low-cut bodice that she favoured—a beautiful woman who knew exactly how to use her attributes. For the first time in her entire life Isobel wished that she knew such feminine tricks as she watched the exchange.

'I shall be returning to France before the winter begins, Lady Anne.'

'To other battles?'

He nodded. 'Philip has his enemies.'

'But you have at least slain one of David's, my lord, for the Ceann Gronna keep is finally loyal. It must be a relief, Lady Dalceann, to be welcomed back into the fold?'

Could Anne of Kinburn possibly be asking that question in innocence? Her keep lost and many of her men with it, their blood on flagstones running red with death.

'Relief is not the word I would use, Lady Anne.'

'Gratitude, then, perhaps, Lady Dalceann?'

Isobel remained quiet, catching the flat green of Marc's eyes, warning away anger.

'Let me go.' A voice above all the others in the room suddenly took her attention and she saw Catriona McQuarry trying to extricate her hand from a tall and well-built man.

The fellow seemed to have no mind to listen as he all but dragged her up from her seat at the table and towards the door. Everyone else around them ignored her obvious panic, watching with the look of people who did not want to get involved in a fuss.

'Catriona McQuarry is always creating a scene,' Anne of Kinburn observed, picking up a crust of bread and dipping it in the sauce still left on her plate.

'I think a strong man would do her the world of good. Perhaps this one is him.'

Others laughed, those closer to the action egging on the unexpected show. Isobel noticed that his fingers left marks on the pale skin of her forearm. Even the minstrel playing his harp at the other end of the room stopped his tune in interest.

Catriona was a woman who had not cultivated her own physical strength and who did not understand the tricks even a small adversary might use to free themselves. Nae, she did not attack at all as she should have done.

Without a moment's thought Isobel stood and marched across to the door that they were making for. 'Lady Catriona is telling you that she wishes to be set free.'

When the man failed to take any notice at all she simply leant across and twisted his other arm in the way Ian had shown her so many times in the bailey at Ceann Gronna. Yelping with pain, the man spun back, his feet getting tangled up with those of a bench behind him and landing hard on his backside.

Catriona was shaking now, her fingers clamped across Isobel's arm as if the whole world depended on it.

'Nobody shall make you go where you do not wish to, Lady Catriona.'

As the silence lengthened Isobel simply took her hand and led her from the room.

* * *

'God.' Marc swore beneath his breath, watching the scene play out before him, for Isobel had just given Huntworth all the reasons in the world to hate her. He knew the man to be one of the McQuarry minions, even if Isobel so plainly did not, and the silence in the chamber was beginning to be punctuated by small whispered conjecture as the court tried to make sense of it all.

'Does Lady Dalceann not fear retribution?' Anne of Kinburn's voice came through the growing chatter, a sense of regard plain in the tone.

'I think she could handle it if it did come,' the man beside him returned.

'Catriona McQuarry has never been the same since her marriage. What did Isobel Dalceann do to MacDougal's arm?'

'It's the witchcraft, mayhap, for I have never seen such a reaction from so small a touch.'

All over the room people looked towards the door, hoping Isobel might reappear, the fear of a throng mesmerised by the unexpected. Marc leant back, the anger in him kept under restraint by sheer will. Did Isobel Dalceann never take her own safety into consideration and was it for ever up to him to do so?

A buzz of something akin to alarm swept the room, the sort of feeling, he imagined, that would vibrate in a cornfield amongst the mice when a hungry hawk hovered above them searching for dinner.

Isobel Dalceann was as magnificent as she was lethal and the hold she had placed on the man waylaying Lady Catriona was one he had never seen before. The fellow still shook his hand even now, a brace of moments later, his fingers red rigid with the numbed shock of touch.

He wanted to laugh and rise to follow, but he knew to do that would incite the questions he so very dearly wished to avoid. People must perceive his indifference, if he was to be of any help to her at all here in Edinburgh.

Hence he raised his glass and turned to the table.

'To bravery,' he toasted, hoping that the words might change agitation into respect, even as he began to eat the meat from the plate placed before him.

'Stuart knows I gave you the ring.' Catriona sat on the bed, doing her best to collect herself. 'I must be right and there is some connection between the McQuarrys and de Courtenay that they do not wish to be made known.' The sun had fallen down at least an hour's worth of minutes and yet still she shook.

'No one will hurt you, Catriona, for I will not allow it.'

Renewed anguish filled the room. 'That is the difference between us, don't you see? I used to be like you once and now...' The breath was forced from her body, leaving her face a violent red as she gasped for air.

'But you are brave. Few others would have risked the wrath of the McQuarrys by showing me the ring.'

Hope surged in the older woman's eyes, making her beautiful. 'I had forgotten what hope was until you came to Edinburgh, Isobel, but for now I will repair to my father's home in the north of Scotland. I can no longer be certain of my own safety in Edinburgh, you see, though if you have need of a place of sanctuary, you would be warmly welcomed there.'

'At this moment I am under the will of the king, but perhaps in time…'

Isobel liked the way Catriona squeezed her hand in friendship as the king's servant came into the room to bid the older woman follow him into the company of David. A monarch ruled well by knowing all the factions of his court, she supposed, and hoped Catriona's father's influence would be enough to give her safety.

Marc waited outside, leaning against the wall, two of the king's men hovering a little way off, watching him with interest. He pushed himself away from the smoothed stone when he saw her.

'Would a stroll suit you, Lady Dalceann?'

The look on his face confused her. The man inside with detachment and indifference in his eyes was long gone. A barely contained fury stood there now, the muscles in his jaw moving under the pressure of what he held within.

She was pleased the garden was deserted when they reached it, a cool wind whipping up her skirts. Her hands bunched the material to keep it stable as she waited for him to speak.

'There are certain rules in a place like the royal court which are wise to observe. Not angering those who hold the power to hurt you is one such canon.' Every word was enunciated with care, his accent barely noticeable.

'You speak of Catriona McQuarry, no doubt. The man was dragging her off against her will and—'

He did not let her finish.

'The man was one of Stuart McQuarry's henchmen and safety here in Edinburgh lies in appearing to be exactly the person you are not.'

With the sun on his hair, gilded in the light, he looked nothing like the warlord everyone here tiptoed around, the very embodiment of his skewered theory. Suddenly Isobel had had all she could take of trying to understand him.

'And how well you do that! You are not a Huntworth, yet the old Earl held a box of mementos with your name on every one. You are not of royal blood, yet the ring you wear holds the crest of the Valois family of Burgundy. A cloth seller. A man of the sword. A betrayer. A lover. An enforcer of the king's will only for coin whilst still believing in the innate justice of law.' She laughed, but the sound was hard and brittle. 'You are so many things, Marc de

Courtenay, that you have forgotten just who it is you really are.'

The green in his eyes was the colour of the Scots pine at Ceann Gronna, trees that hung dark and ragged on the northern ridge.

'Oh, I know exactly who I am. I am a bastard. My mother was wooed briefly by a stranger who then quit France, leaving her to die from the shame of it all. Her name was Beatrice and she was a second cousin of the king, too innocent to understand that the words and actions of a travelling Scottish nobleman were so very false. That is the sort of men you deal with here, Isobel, all alone in a roomful of strangers; men who strike out for their own chance and be damned to whom they ruin in the process. They will see your isolation and be pleased by it—such an easy target with your father a crazed dissenter and your keep the subject of many a jester's tale.'

Only myth and hearsay! She was disappointed by his arguments. 'Then I will die fighting with justice and righteousness at my side.'

He shook his head, his voice lower now and threaded with a flat certainty. 'Nae. You will die in little pieces like Catriona McQuarry has or like my mother did, because men such as Huntworth do not deal in small deaths or quick payments.'

'The king will already know of how Stuart McQuarry's man hurt Catriona. Her father is powerful, too.'

'And for a while he might listen, until the heavy clink of coinage saying otherwise deafens his ears.'

'McQuarry would bribe him for my hand in marriage?' Her voice rose with the horror of it.

'Without a doubt he will. And the court will remember you as that untutored Dalceann woman who needed a strict lesson from a powerful lord in the obligations of a wife.'

'I do not believe you.'

'Ask Lady Catriona, then, for such a truth.'

Isobel turned from him, trying to sort out just what it was he said. Lord, the intrigue in her keep in Fife was nothing as compared to here and everything he said was beginning to settle.

She was a novice in the games that Marc had played for years on the stage of kings and the theatres of war and she understood in that second just exactly what she had done.

She had implicated him in all of this as surely as she was involved. No wonder he was so angry.

'I release you then from any duty you feel towards my welfare, Sir Marcus.'

He caught her arm and held it, not softly, either. 'Such acquittance, Lady Dalceann, and such a lie. There can be no such easy release from what burns between us and you damn well know it.'

Further afield a group of people wandered down a pathway into their view and above them on the parapet the guards would no doubt be watching. Edinburgh had eyes and ears at every turn. This was no place at all for saying more.

'Keep your knife in hand and do not walk into the dark spaces of the castle.'

With that he was gone, through the gateway that led to the outer courtyard, his back broad and straight. She watched the sunlight play on his figure, tall and graceful as he threaded his way through a group of well-dressed lords and ladies.

Chapter Seventeen

The lack of sleep was starting to tell on him as the headache Marc had felt building all day pounded in his brow. Three nights of sentry duty watching the gateway into the chambers of Lady Isobel Dalceann was turning into a fourth and the crook of the tree he sat in amidst the gardens was no longer as comfortable as it had been on the first night. But Isobel was in the most danger in the small morning hours when the castle slept and those with ill intent had more leeway to creep hidden under shadow.

Swiping his hair back from his forehead, he massaged his temple with swift strokes. Another few hours and it would be safer. Another few hours and he could sleep.

The shape of someone in the half-light had him up and out of the garden, his knife drawn in readiness, although sheer and utter amazement confounded him when he saw it to be Isobel Dalceann herself beckoning.

He reached her in under three breath-falls.

'What the hell are you doing out of your room?'

'Finding you,' she replied, her hair tousled and her cheeks flushed. 'You have been missing from the court and today I saw Mariner and asked him why.'

'He should have damn well said nothing.' He looked around, but not a thing moved, the moonlight full and exposing. Taking a breath, he calmed himself even as she spoke.

'Can we talk?'

'Not here.'

'In my room, then?'

His body stiffened at such a request. God, he wanted her so much he barely trusted himself to be alone with her, but a meeting inside would be so much more secure.

'Please?'

It was the entreaty that did it and he followed her up the stairs and into her chamber, making certain the door behind them was well locked. Linking his hands behind his back, he stood there, waiting.

'You were right. The court is more dangerous when they are uncertain of you.' Her voice was soft and tired. 'They think I am a witch again. Even David watches me now.'

'A witch?' He echoed the word and smiled. 'Perhaps that will help you, then. The black arts make cowards of those who believe in them.'

'Do you believe in them?'

He shook his head. 'I am a soldier and there is enough sorcery in that.'

Their eyes met and held across the small space; he felt solace in her strength.

'If I were to simply disappear, would David punish those left at Ceann Gronna because of it?'

How often had he asked himself that very same question and come up without an answer? If he knew for certain the king would be kind, he would have had Isobel out of Edinburgh in a second. But he didn't.

'I could not live, you see, if the Dalceann name were to be lost for my freedom. It would be no life to tread on the graves of those I loved.'

'There is still time to change the king's mind before he orders a betrothal, and even a day can make a difference in the politics of a court.'

'You see a way out of this? For us?'

Us. The word rocked him. Lord, how much he wanted an *us*.

'There is always a way to get what you want. A trip has been arranged to Dunfermline at the end of the week as an interlude for the royal party. Huntworth will use the outing to attempt to kill me.'

'How do you know all that?'

'I've led armies across Europe and lived with kings. Every court has its own systems of intelligence and this one is no different.'

'How will he try it?

'On the water. He will probably use the summer sea mists to hide in.'

'Then the king must be told of such treachery before it is allowed to happen.'

He tipped back his head and laughed, the sweet sound of her worry balanced against this one chance of retribution.

'No, Isobel,' he said finally as he caught his breath. 'We must allow Stuart McQuarry all the room in the world to disgrace himself.'

He was so beautiful, Isobel thought, the stubble on his cheeks catching the brightness of the moon. Mariner had told her today of Marc watching her chamber by night to make certain she was safe. Her protector. Her saviour. She could never remember feeling like this in the company of any other man before and now the fear of losing him to a madman bent on murder made her stomach feel sick.

Stepping forwards she caught his hand and held it tight, the warmth and the strength of him comforting against the truth he had given her—a rare gift in a court filled with lies. She liked the way his fingers tightened against her own.

'McQuarry must believe there is some truth in what Catriona said to want to kill you.'

Placing his fingers across the swelling warmth of her breast, she watched him, the thin silk of her nightdress the only thing that separated her from nakedness. If she was going to be married off for the convenience of a king, then she would use the time she had left to understand all that she would never forget.

'Here and now, let there just be us.'

The place between her legs throbbed and her palm fell to his groin, cupping the fullness of him.

'Ahhh, love,' he whispered in reply and turned her face into his. 'We should not, but...'

His lips covered hers, the words between them lost to need, his tongue probing and the world anchored by urgency.

Marc de Courtenay was home in a way Alisdair had never been. It was in his strength and his certainty and the way he strode across life, nothing in his path unshiftable.

Save the suitors.

She shook her head. Not now. She would not think of them now.

'I want you.' He spoke as he hauled her towards him, his back against the wall, the words hardly heard. 'I want you when I wake up in the morning and I need you when I fall into slumber at night.'

He lifted her arms and the pale slip of silk was lost, pooling in shadow on the floor. His eyes ran across everything, the heat in him seen under hooded lids, her breasts jutting in the cool, waiting for his touch.

Only them and only this.

What manner of magic did he use upon her? What force drew them perfectly together, fitting like a new-made glove? Her muscles felt so weak she could barely stand.

I know exactly what to do. I know how to love a man now to the very bottom of my heart.

She almost said it. Almost let the words go to form a new understanding between them, either taken or refused, but she was not brave enough.

Hold him first, her mind said, as she opened her legs to the hand that came forwards, turning into his embrace.

The heat inside, beneath her skin, was the kind that turned into rapture, layered with the knowledge of what had come before and what might follow next. Imprinted. Indescribable.

His touch across the rise of her bottom was gentle as she closed her eyes to simply feel the hard strength of arousal, his breath against her cheek. The smell of a man who did not favour the scents that many of the other men in court plied themselves with.

Only Marc against her body and then inside, drawing her towards ecstasy, thrusting closer and higher, her cries taken into his mouth and lost into their joining.

Her nipples ached as the building waves began to crest, thin pains of perfection calling for bliss.

Her climax came even as she tried to stop it, rolling in to clench every muscle, her breath pulsing tight as she stretched out to feel the fullness.

Taken and consumed. She felt only freedom.

'*Mon Dieu.*' Marc was suddenly still and the control she always saw in his eyes was gone as he looked into her face and emptied his seed inside, no thoughts to break away.

She held him there tightly, wanting the possibility of all he had not given before, and looking directly at him to show him how she felt. She did not let him pull back one tiny bit, as the moon broke through a heavy covering of clouds and came upon them, highlighting his nakedness, dark hair whorling into pattern as a single tear rolled down her cheek. His tongue took it from her before he leaned his forehead against the wall.

'God, Isobel.'

'I love you.'

She had not meant to say those words, but they came anyway, soft into the room like thieves and taking all free will with them.

The link of flesh joining them swelled and she saw surrender in the muscles of his shoulders as he breathed in both pain and pleasure, finely tuned, and answered her back with his body.

An hour later he lay spent beside her in the bed, holding her while she slept and liking the small warmth of breath against his arm.

He could not remember another woman whom he had left his seed inside of his own volition and the thought made his grip tighten, for how well he understood the place given to a bastard child outside of wedlock.

Isobel had said she loved him, in the final rush of pleasure, whispered against his ear as she spun into the realm of sensuality, the nub of her as tight as a drum.

He could not say it back, not yet when the king and his barons all gathered around her with their own plans, for the Dalceann keep or for Isobel it mattered not which. She was a pawn in a game with rules he needed to observe carefully in order to be able to win.

But she was his. He would never let her go.

He felt her breathing change and knew she had awakened.

'What is the time?'

Looking out of the window, he checked the position of the moon. 'Near three, I would guess.' He knew he could not remain much longer.

'Stay another hour.'

No question was implied as she rose on her elbows without a stitch covering her nakedness and her hair tousled. Marc thought that she had never looked more beautiful than she did at that moment.

His!

He smiled because for the first time in all of his life he had met a woman who did not play games when she looked him straight in the eyes and offered him everything.

Chapter Eighteen

She had told Marc de Courtenay that she loved him
and she had barely seen him since, lost in the whirl
of courtly events and David's insistence on her presence at every one of them.

It had been a mistake to say the words, she knew
it had been from the moment she had said them.

I love you.

Lord. Three little words that had him running
scared.

She had heard nothing more from Marc about today's trip on the boats to Dunfermline, though she
knew she was to accompany the king and his party.
Her own sources had informed her Marc would be
travelling over last with his men as company, the information gleaned from a lad she had paid well to
ask. Mariner had been more than forthcoming with
the tidings, a fact that begged another question altogether. She knew that if the de Courtenay camp had
wished for secrecy they would never have said any-

thing, which meant that McQuarry must know of Marcus's movements as well as she did.

Helen Cunningham was uncertain and edgy, the thought of a sea trip making her head ache.

Isobel had brought with her some of the herbs she had drugged Marc with once, in the forest above the sea coast, and it was easy to offer her chaperon a drink to still her fear.

Ten minutes later when Helen was fast asleep, Isobel sent word to the king that the older woman was not well and that she felt it wise to spend the day with her whilst she recovered from her ailment.

She smiled at the thought of such an easy grace of hours as she changed into the lad's clothes brought along for the ruse, a hat pulled hard down on her head and a handful of charcoal from the fireplace smeared into her skin. She now looked like a youth who had neither the wherewithal to bathe nor the inclination, and the cold white sea fog added to deception.

Perfect!

Without a backward glance Isobel departed the room and wound her way down to the shore, the ease of turning from a girl into a boy well practised after many years of wearing hose.

Nobody gave a backward glance to the youth who sauntered past the crafts transporting the royal group to the other side of the bay, an interested onlooker whose figure was then lost to the rolling, early morning mists of the Firth.

* * *

Marc should have known better than to expect an outing of the court to go exactly as it had been planned, and he knew he was in trouble the moment Lady Anne of Kinburn, her husband and two other high-born men and women came to plead for a lift across to Dunfermline, having missed their earlier transportation.

With no other conveyances at the wharf he was unable to refuse without inciting the questions that would later follow should Huntworth not go through with his plans. But he sat them in the back of the boat against the pile of ropes and sailcloths stacked in the aft and well away from the oarsmen he had hand chosen for their strength.

The boat was small, but easily manoeuvred, and with ten of his men aboard and all well armed, he did not think it would be difficult to repel any assault.

'I knew, of course, that we should have come down earlier, but I thought the mist would delay everything.'

Anne of Kinburn's husband did not look at all happy. 'If you had taken a few less hours on your hair, Anne, we might have all been on time.'

The bickering continued until they were out into the middle of the Firth, a good half an hour from the other side.

Then, when the sea mists thickened and the waves became choppier, all hell broke loose.

* * *

Isobel could see Marc standing with his soldiers not twelve feet away, his outline blurred even at that distance by a rolling fog. Excitement vied with fear and she pulled her cap down further and repositioned the canvas covering that she hid beneath, the small scar on her palm coming into view as she did so.

Protection. Caught to each other like the sea to the shore, two parts of a whole. Her fist closed about the knife she held and she squinted her eyes to try to make out any craft coming in through the whiteness.

It came out of nowhere, some few moments later, ramming them without any compunction.

Isobel felt the lurch of it, the scrape and then the breaking of timber, splintering under pressure.

Scrambling up from her hiding place under the sailcloth, she came face to face with Anne of Kinburn, her mouth forming a soundless scream and her husband and friends rigid on the seats they had been assigned.

Bearing her knife, she pushed past them, most of the damage to the boat done at the front where Marc and his men stood, swords drawn, a tight circle of deadly intent.

'Stay down,' she shouted at Anne and her group, 'and move to the very back.'

The small party did exactly as they were told, the sobs of the two women present loud and very frightened.

McQuarry's men came in a swarm, leaping on to the boat with the sure footedness of sailors well used to the sway of the sea. Isobel took the first man out even as he came towards her, using the motion of the waves to unbalance him.

Marc shouted and she looked up, another coming from the side. Without haste she jabbed at his thigh, watching as he, too, fell backwards into the water, losing purchase.

The whole front of the boat was now full of fighting men, the noise of blades meeting loud in the morning stillness.

She could see Marc fighting his way back to her, his strokes as sure as the ones she had seen at Ceann Gronna. He left only death in his wake.

When he reached her side he grabbed her by the arm, placing her behind him so that any other threat was lessened, his eyes the greenest she had ever seen them.

'How the hell did you get here?'

She did not have time to answer as another craft came through the mist at full speed towards them, Stuart McQuarry at the helm shouting out instructions. Marc's arm around her chest held her to him as the jolt ripped through the boat, his grip knocked away by the broken remains of a flying oar which gouged deep into his flesh.

He had been hit, the blood from his forearm dripping down on to Isobel, the cap she had worn flown off in the jolt, so that the heavy plait of her hair draped across him.

He could not believe she was here, in danger with the bastard Huntworth upon them and revenge in his eyes. Anne of Kinburn was screaming now as she turned over and over in the air to plop into the sea like a great jellyfish, her skirts filling, yellow against the slate grey of ocean.

Mariner was down, too—hit by the collision, Marc hoped, and not pierced by a blade. Further off in the water two of the others in the Kinburn party floundered, the ocean pulling them under with ease.

He had not expected the second ship, had not been ready for it; he, who usually looked for every contingency at the head of armies, had failed to do so here.

Why?

Because his whole focus had shifted to Isobel when he had seen her in danger. He did not want to let her go still, with the unfolding horror all around him. He wanted to keep her here behind him and safe, her warmth soft against everything brutal. If she died, he would, too. It was that simple. Isobel Dalceann with her spirit and bravery had taken his heart and made it her own.

God! The thought floored him as surely as the battle, the beat of blood in his temples pounding hard.

'I love you, too.' Said as he turned her head around to his lips and kissed her fast and quick, his sword arm raised against any other intrusion.

He saw her eyes widen in surprise even as the dimples in her cheeks rounded, the blood from his arm reddening her tunic and noise all about them.

One moment of love snatched against a cauldron of hate in the midst of battle. He smiled because with all that had gone before it was appropriate somehow, this centre of calm within a vortex of chaos.

And then she was gone, across the side of the boat into the water and swimming hard for the shrieking Anne of Kinburn.

He loved her. He had kissed her in front of everyone and had meant what he said. Joy rang in all the parts of Isobel's body. She saw him now with his sword flashing, an expert against novices; how very easy he made it all look.

'Please keep him safe,' she prayed in a whisper, for if she was to lose him when he had proclaimed his feelings… No, she would not think of that.

She reached Anne and hauled her up, holding her face above the water.

'Keep still and I will take you back to the boat,' she ordered, pulling with an easy side-crawl towards it. Anne to her credit listened, and it was only a moment or so until she was back against the railing of wood.

'Stay beneath the rim. It will be safer. Just hold on while I get the others.'

'My h-h-husband?' Her teeth chattered alarmingly, the wimpled hat she wore filled with water and dragging behind. With a quick flick of her knife Isobel cut the ties and then she was off again, the white of the mist hiding the others further away, but their cries alerting her to their positions.

Marc could not see Isobel anywhere and the dread of her absence was building. Huntworth was less than a few feet away, his men depleted by the skirmish, the second boat sitting against the ocean at an angle that suggested it was taking on water and fast. Eight of the enemy left against their six. Easy odds. Stepping forwards he met Stuart McQuarry head on.

'This is for my brother, de Courtenay, for his blood on your hands at Ceann Gronna.'

Marc laughed and the sound was not humorous. 'Oh, he was a dead man long before that, hose around his knees in shame, an easy conquest with his pretensions and his greed—a familial characteristic, perhaps?'

The other snarled. 'You come to Scotland with your patronage from the French king and inveigle your way into the heart of the court, an impostor and a bastard.' His sword swung sharp and Marc parried. He did not wish to kill him yet for there were things he needed to know.

'Some here say my father was a Scottish earl. Your own, perhaps?'

He smiled as rage reddened the face of the one opposite.

'Lady Catriona has been loose of tongue, no doubt, with her dubious truths and her filtered reality.' Stuart McQuarry stopped to catch breath as he brought his blade down hard, the snap of it chilling.

Marc waited. The truth was close, he could feel it, he only needed to keep him talking.

'She says there is proof.'

The whites of Huntworth's eyes made him look more crazed than ever.

'My father paid your aunt to keep you away from us, a memory that we did not want to come knocking at our door, and the plan worked until Philip sent you here and you began to snoop.'

'So you are my brother?' Marc was winded by the horror of this truth.

'No. Your cousin. Quinlan, my father's youngest brother, wanted you here amongst us, a child who had connections with the royal court of France. He was the dead wood on the family tree.'

'So you killed him?' The battle around was dimmer now, the truth of what he was hearing making it so.

'Someone had to save the Huntworth name from being a laughing-stock. Archibald and I decided to.'

Marc swore. It was enough. He had heard enough.

'Tell your brothers and father that you have failed in your quest, then, when you reach hell.'

With one parry he buried his blade into the heart of his cousin and watched the light fade from his eyes.

A moment later it was all over, the last Huntworth supporter dumped overboard to sink into the arms of the ocean.

One of his men had Anne of Kinburn, pulling her aboard easily from the place where she hung, half in and half out of the water. Her husband and his friend joined her, streams of cold flowing from their clothes. But the other woman was missing and so was Isobel.

Ten minutes since she had jumped overboard, Marc surmised, looking wildly around.

'Isobel.' He shouted her name and listened for an answer, the others on the craft doing the same. The mist had thickened and he could not make out an outline of anything.

'Isobel.'

Still silence.

Stripping off his shoes, he dived into the water, stroking around the rim of the boat to see that she was not there hanging on and unable to reply.

There was nothing, so he set out further, his arms aching with the crawl of cold and the pain of the splinter which had pierced him.

He could not believe it.

'Isobel. Isobel. Isobel.' He called till his voice was rough and hoarse, the waves bigger now, dunking him under and making him cough. Still he stroked back and forth, his legs kicking the murky depths below in the hope of feeling her there and for the first time in his life he cried, the warm tears mixing with freezing salt and running down his cheeks like a child.

When he had lost Guy it felt nothing like this, nothing like this tearing pain of agony choking away life. Fisting his hand, he waved it at the heavens and screamed his anger.

The boat came out of the mist and he caught the side, swinging himself inside in one easy movement and ordering the oarsmen this way and that.

Anne of Kinburn was crying, the sound annoying him with all it implied. Mariner had recovered from his knock on the head, but he did not look at all well. The rest of his men sat as sentries for any sign of life as they trawled the water, up and down, up and down.

Four hours later he knew he had lost her, the Firth of Forth so frigid there could be no survival in such a temperature.

Nothing made sense any more—the soaked red sleeve of his kirtle, his lack of breath, the sun finally breaking through the mist and filling the ocean with emptiness.

Another boat had pulled alongside them, taking Anne, her husband and friend and Mariner with some of his men.

He refused to leave the craft, however, as the oarsmen agreed to look further.

By nightfall he knew he could search no more and with utter grief he gestured for the men to return to the wharf they had left a good ten hours earlier.

Chapter Nineteen

The people were kind and their fire was warm. Lady Linda Carr sat beside her crying, the blush on her face filled with pity.

'I am sorry, Lady Dalceann, but I could not stop them.'

Isobel tried to focus her eyes on all that was happening about her. She knew she had reached the shore late in the night, dragging the big woman with her, but it had all seemed a blur after that.

Wriggling her toes and her fingers, she tried to work out what it was Lady Carr spoke of. She could still see, move and hear. The list went on as she tested various parts of her body.

'Your hair is gone,' the woman wailed as Isobel's hands reached up. 'It was caught in the wooden piles and they could not free you, so they cut it off to bring you up from the sea.'

Isobel felt the shorn tufts of her hair, the end of

her tresses feeling strange and ragged. 'It does not matter.'

Her rescuer, his wife and two young children huddled to one side.

She tried to sit up but a pain sliced across her temple so she lay back again, waiting till her vision cleared.

'Where are we?'

Lady Carr was not certain and turned to the corner. The man stood, doffing his head at them as if they were great royalty. For the first time Isobel saw that Linda was draped in a blanket and that beneath the covers of the bed all she wore was a cotton shift.

'Ye are in a village just north of Edinburgh, my lady. I am a fisherman and found you as I made to bring my boat up on to the hard. It has just come dawn so I will send word to your people. The lady here tells me that you were part of the king's party making for Dunfermline.' Again he bowed his head.

Marc. Lord, he must be frantic by now if he had managed to repel the Huntworth attack. She hardly dared ask the next question.

'Were other people found?'

'Two bodies of soldiers, my lady. The lady here did not recognise either.'

Lady Carr began to sob. 'Oh, it was so terrible. I couldn't look upon their poor faces, for they seemed—'

Isobel cut across the top of her and addressed the

man. 'Can you take us back to Edinburgh in your boat? I will make certain it is worth your while.'

She tried to sit up, the movement making her dizzy and sick.

'I think it best if you stay lying down,' Lady Carr said, 'for your face is paper white.'

'No. I need to be on that boat.' Her legs felt like jelly as she hung them across the side of the bed, the earth cold and smooth beneath her bare feet. The two children watched her with enormous eyes as Linda laid the blanket about her shoulders. With her head thumping and her stomach turning, Isobel stood, collecting her clothes from the end of the bed and slowly following the woman out of the back door to a small room away from the house which would afford her some privacy to dress herself.

Marc wandered towards the wharf like a wraith. He had not slept and the dawn could not come fast enough for him to take out another craft and look for Isobel.

He felt the eyes of everyone upon him, his arm pulled up into a sling and his left eye swollen. Huntworth might have left his mark on him, but the injuries inside were the ones that ached.

Isobel.

He wanted her. He wanted to feel her beside him as they marched into their future together. He wanted to love her until he was old and all their children had grown.

Now the past reached out again and grabbed him, again, the lonely life of the army, a man with no home save that in battle.

Mariner joined him as he covered the final yards on the wharf.

'More bodies washed up this morning, but she was not amongst them.' Hope flared and then dimmed. There were so many places, after all, that the currents could carry the drowned. 'The king has sent word he will return this morning. It seems everyone in the court is in shock over McQuarry's blatancy.'

He nodded, but he did not really listen. He did not care for the shock of others, removed as they were from the loss he knew. He did not want the king milling around him or the pity that he perceived here on the wharf amongst his own men.

All he wanted was her, Isobel, soft and warm and brave in his arms.

He remembered the last time he had seen her diving free into the water, unafraid, certain, the strong stroke of her arms lost in the mist even as he watched her go. She had brought back Lady Anne of Kinburn and her husband and his friend, but Linda Carr was still lost and Geoffrey Kinburn had intimated that the woman had been panicking. Marc's memory of her was that of a large female. Had Isobel tried to calm her, had she attempted to bring her back, only to be pulled under by a stronger force? He shook his head and took in a breath.

No. He could not do this and live; he had to be at his best to find her again.

She was going to be sick. It was the motion of the sea and the dizziness in her head and the cold of the dawn rising slowly.

Her fingers closed white around the seat beneath her, wishing away nausea and the shaking that had begun as they had made their way to the shore, which had worsened considerably.

Simon, the stranger they had pulled from the water at Fife Ness, came to mind as she tried to still the chattering of her teeth and she closed her eyes against the memory.

'Ahoy there!' The fisherman's voice was loud and, drawing herself up, she watched as the shape of another boat materialised a good two hundred yards away, the mist this morning light and patchy.

'We are saved.' Linda Carr began to shout out, her voice drifting across the water, the answering calls of other voices vying with it and a horn sounding.

Isobel's heart started to pound. It was him. She knew that it was, coming through the first light to find her.

'It's a boat,' Mariner observed, 'with three people in it.'

'A woman. One of them is a woman.' Marc could

see the bright swathe of gown on a figure that was large and rounded. Lady Linda Carr, perhaps? His eyes searched out the smaller outline next to her, looking for the long plait of hair.

His heart sank. A youth it seemed crouched beside the other as the boat came closer, dark hair cropped in the fashion preferred by the young pages and the only other occupant a fisherman by the looks, one of the many who plied this part of the Firth.

He let out the breath he was holding. Lord, that the one Isobel had gone to rescue had survived while she had perished; the very wrongness of it made anger turn.

Forty yards away now, then thirty.

Then there she was, Isobel, after all, white faced and staring, all words gone and lost as their eyes took in each other.

A miracle.

The noise of cheering was around him as the boat came aside and he felt his hand reach out and take hers, small and cold, lifting her over to him, her shaking body fitting beneath his cloak, her head under his chin lain against his heart and safe.

Everything felt warmer—the heavy wool of his cape wrapping her in heat, his body hard against her own, his hands holding on as if he might never let her go again.

'Where the hell were you?' he whispered in her ear. 'I have looked everywhere.'

The bandage on his left arm was thick.

'Trying to get back to you.' She had promised she would not cry, but now she did, her sobs almost as noisy as those of Lady Carr. She could not care. She had had enough of bravery and strength. All that was left was honesty.

'Ah, love,' he whispered, running his free hand through her shortened hair and she looked up.

'They...c-cut it to s-save me.' Vanity in the eye of the storm was so very unheroic, but he did not seem to be worrying, the smile in his eyes bright and true.

'Is Stuart McQuarry dead?' She needed to know that he was gone and that the episode at sea would not be repeated.

'He is.'

'I l-love y-you.' Spoken through her shaking sobs.

Around them Isobel could see Mariner and the rest of his men listening, along with Lady Carr, who had finally ceased to cry, and five other soldiers from the court of David.

Was it dangerous to make such a proclamation? Would there be consequences even now? Closing her eyes, she simply rested against the danger because, in this very second, she was home.

They were summoned to the court the next morning for a session with the king.

Everyone was there when they arrived—no small number, either, leaving a passageway for them to travel through, hundreds of lords and ladies dressed in their very best.

Even the trumpeters sounded as they walked, the colours of David draped in long banners on the walls around them. The room had been decorated with other banners, too, she noticed, more festive and richly embellished. Every person that they passed was smiling.

David rose when they stopped before him, his gown of ermine and red undeniably luxurious. All Isobel could think of was the suitors. Was it today she would be torn away from Marc into a marriage?

'You came to our court as the vanquished daughter of Ceann Gronna, Lady Dalceann, and you stand now as the saviour of four people with the loftiest names in Edinburgh.'

The Kinburns, who she had not noticed, stepped forwards as did Lady Linda Carr and her husband, all acknowledging the debt they owed to her by bowing low.

'I said that I should give you the month to choose a suitor of good name and family. But I rescind that promise now. I wish to choose for you, and the man who will be yours will henceforth be an earl of my court and the head of an old and venerable family name.'

Isobel turned to catch Marc's eyes, but he was

not looking at her. His hands were tight fists at his side. Please God, let them not have come this far to be denied each other now! She bit down on protest as the king went on.

'Step forwards, Sir Marc de Courtenay.'

Against the king Marc looked tall and broad, his hair pulled back and slicked with water.

'You came to Edinburgh on a promise from the King of France and you have given good loyalty and service here, for which I thank you. There is another matter entirely, however, that I wish to pursue with you now. It is said that Stuart McQuarry, the Earl of Huntworth, is dead, his ill-made attempt on your life yesterday costing him and his men dearly. My own findings show that there is still one McQuarry heir left, however, a man who could take the title through his father's name and use it wisely. That man is you, Lord Marc, the Earl of Huntworth.'

The crowd was as surprised as Isobel. Was what he was saying proven beyond doubt? She waited as Marc began to speak.

'Then as the Earl I should like to put my name forwards as a suitor for Lady Isobel Dalceann.'

The king began to smile. 'Isobel Dalceann, would you accept marriage with this man?'

'Indeed I would, sir. He is exactly the husband that I want.'

Three hours later the celebrations were still in full swing, the marriage of the new Earl of Huntworth to Isobel Dalceann a party that many would remember for years.

Not a betrothal of convenience or politics or for the greed of possessions, but a marriage for love. Everyone came forward to offer them their most sincere and hearty best wishes.

Much later they lay in each other's arms, the joy of for ever lingering in the kiss between them.

A full moon in a cloudless sky bathed the room in light and the fire in the hearth chased away the cold.

'Thank the Lord you are a fine swimmer, Isobel. I should have known it after you brought me in through the waves on the beach at Fife Ness.'

She wriggled against him, her finger tracing the sensitive skin about his nipple.

'After five hours I thought of simply giving up and letting the sea take me, but your love drew me on.'

'If I had lost you…' He let the words go because he could not imagine what he might qualify such a statement with.

'You will never lose me because I love you, Marc.'

Turning into his beautiful wife's warmth, he knew everything was right in his world and that finally he had found his place. Aye, the keep at Ceann Gronna and the castle at Stirling would ring with the sound of their children and their children's children.

Opening his palm, he laid it across her breast. 'I give you my heart to keep, Isobel, always and for ever.'

When she smiled back he thought he had never seen her look more beautiful.

* * * * *

REQUEST YOUR FREE BOOKS!

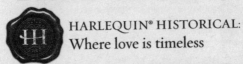

HARLEQUIN® HISTORICAL:
Where love is timeless

2 FREE NOVELS PLUS 2 FREE GIFTS!

YES! Please send me 2 FREE Harlequin® Historical novels and my 2 FREE gifts (gifts are worth about \$10). After receiving them, if I don't wish to receive any more books, I can return the shipping statement marked "cancel." If I don't cancel, I will receive 6 brand-new novels every month and be billed just \$5.19 per book in the U.S. or \$5.74 per book in Canada. That's a savings of at least 17% off the cover price! It's quite a bargain! Shipping and handling is just 50¢ per book in the U.S. and 75¢ per book in Canada.* I understand that accepting the 2 free books and gifts places me under no obligation to buy anything. I can always return a shipment and cancel at any time. Even if I never buy another book, the two free books and gifts are mine to keep forever.

246/349 HDN FEQQ

Name	(PLEASE PRINT)	
Address		Apt. #
City	State/Prov.	Zip/Postal Code

Signature (if under 18, a parent or guardian must sign)

Mail to the **Reader Service:**
IN U.S.A.: P.O. Box 1867, Buffalo, NY 14240-1867
IN CANADA: P.O. Box 609, Fort Erie, Ontario L2A 5X3

Not valid for current subscribers to Harlequin Historical books.

Want to try two free books from another line?
Call 1-800-873-8635 or visit www.ReaderService.com.

* Terms and prices subject to change without notice. Prices do not include applicable taxes. Sales tax applicable in N.Y. Canadian residents will be charged applicable taxes. Offer not valid in Quebec. This offer is limited to one order per household. All orders subject to credit approval. Credit or debit balances in a customer's account(s) may be offset by any other outstanding balance owed by or to the customer. Please allow 4 to 6 weeks for delivery. Offer available while quantities last.

Your Privacy—The Reader Service is committed to protecting your privacy. Our Privacy Policy is available online at www.ReaderService.com or upon request from the Reader Service.

We make a portion of our mailing list available to reputable third parties that offer products we believe may interest you. If you prefer that we not exchange your name with third parties, or if you wish to clarify or modify your communication preferences, please visit us at www.ReaderService.com/consumerschoice or write to us at Reader Service Preference Service, P.O. Box 9062, Buffalo, NY 14269. Include your complete name and address.

HHI1B

**All his good intentions are tossed asunder
with one simple touch....**

A DARING AND SENSUAL TALE FROM AUTHOR
TERRI BRISBIN

Ciara Robertson has loved formidable highlander
Tavis MacLerie all her life. Now, *finally* of marriageable
age, Ciara throws her heart at his feet, only to be left
brokenhearted. Tavis knows that innocent Ciara thinks she's
in love with him—but she deserves better. Painful experience
has proved that he's a far better warrior than husband, and
he's determined never to marry again...until he is ordered to
take her to the Murray clan and her new betrothed! Every step
of their long, tormenting journey tempts him more...for he's
coming closer to losing his heart and Ciara forever...

*The Highlanders
Stolen Touch*

Tempt the forbidden this September 2012!

*The mischievously witty Bronwyn Scott
introduces a brand-new trilogy,*
RAKES BEYOND REDEMPTION.

*Three deliciously naughty books, with three equally
devilish rakes. They are far too wicked for polite society...
but these ladies just can't stay away!*

*Read on for a sneak peek of book one
HOW TO DISGRACE A LADY.*

Available in September 2012 from Harlequin® Historical.

"You're a beautiful woman, Alixe Burke."

She stiffened. "You shouldn't say things you don't mean."

"Do you doubt me? Or do you doubt yourself? Don't you think you're beautiful? Surely you're not naive enough to overlook your natural charms."

She turned to face him, forcing him to relinquish his hold. "I'm not naive. I'm a realist."

Merrick shrugged a shoulder as if to say he didn't think much of realism. "What has realism taught you, Alixe?" He folded his arms, waiting to see what she would say next.

"It has taught me that I'm an end to male means. I'm a dowry, a stepping stone for some ambitious man. It's not very flattering."

He could not refute her arguments. There *were* men who saw women that way. But he could refute the hardness in her sherry eyes, eyes that should have been warm. For all her protestations of realism, she was too untried by the world for the measure of cynicism she showed. "What of romance and love? What has realism taught you about those things?"

"If those things exist, they don't exist for me." Alixe's chin went up a fraction in defiance of his probe.

"Is that a dare, Alixe? If it is, I'll take it." Merrick took advantage of their privacy, closing the short distance between them with a touch; the back of his hand reaching out to stroke the curve of her cheek. "A world without romance is a bland world indeed, Alixe. One for which I think you are ill suited." He saw the pulse at the base of her neck leap at the words, the hardness in her eyes soften, curiosity replacing the doubt whether she willed it or not. He let his eyes catch hers then drop to linger on the fullness of her mouth before he drew her to him, whispering, "Let me show you the possibilities." A most seductive invitation to sin.

Don't miss book one of this seductive new trilogy
HOW TO DISGRACE A LADY

Available in September 2012 from Harlequin® Historical.

And watch out for:

HOW TO RUIN A REPUTATION
Available October 2012

HOW TO SIN SUCCESSFULLY
Available November 2012

HHEXP0912